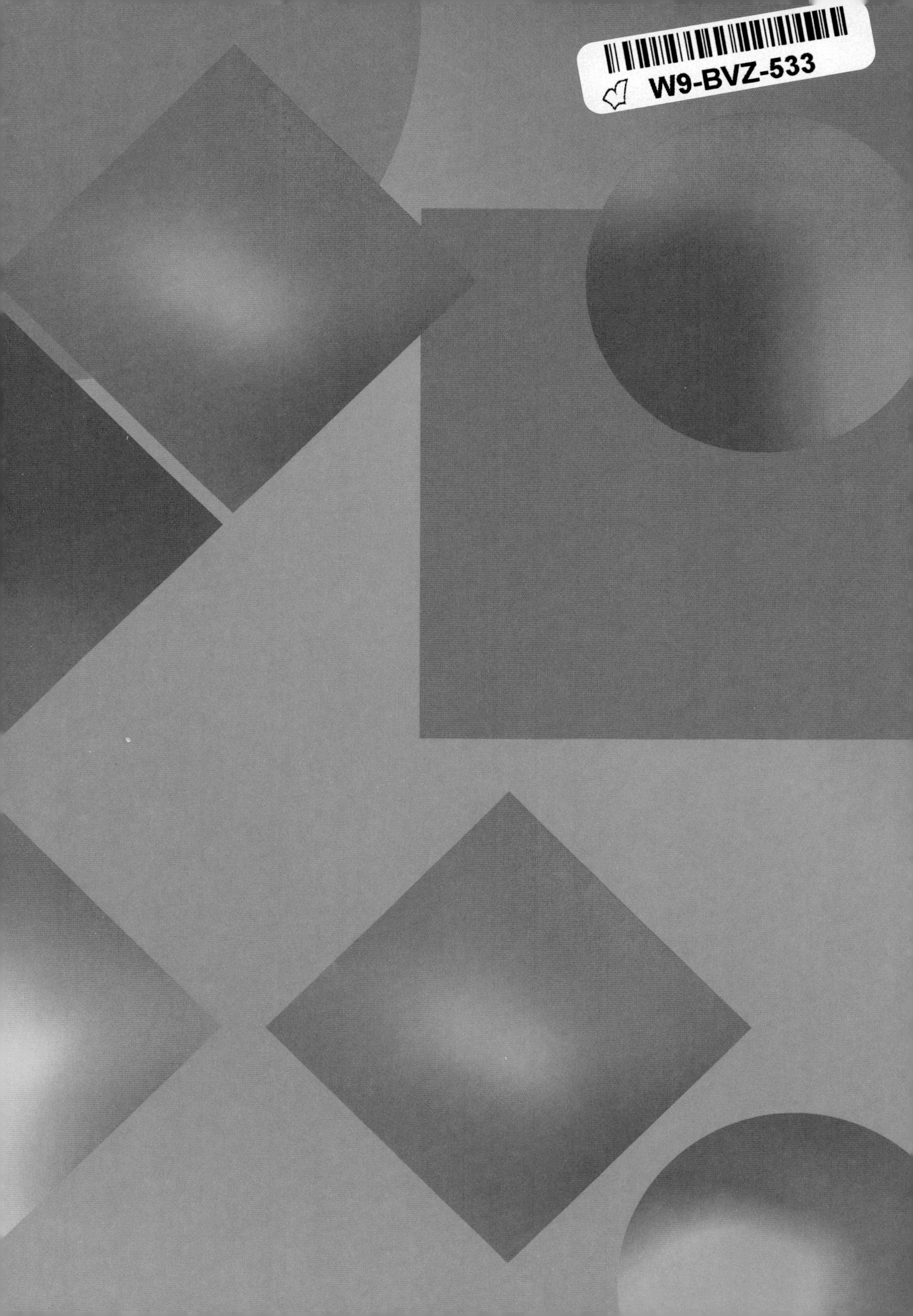

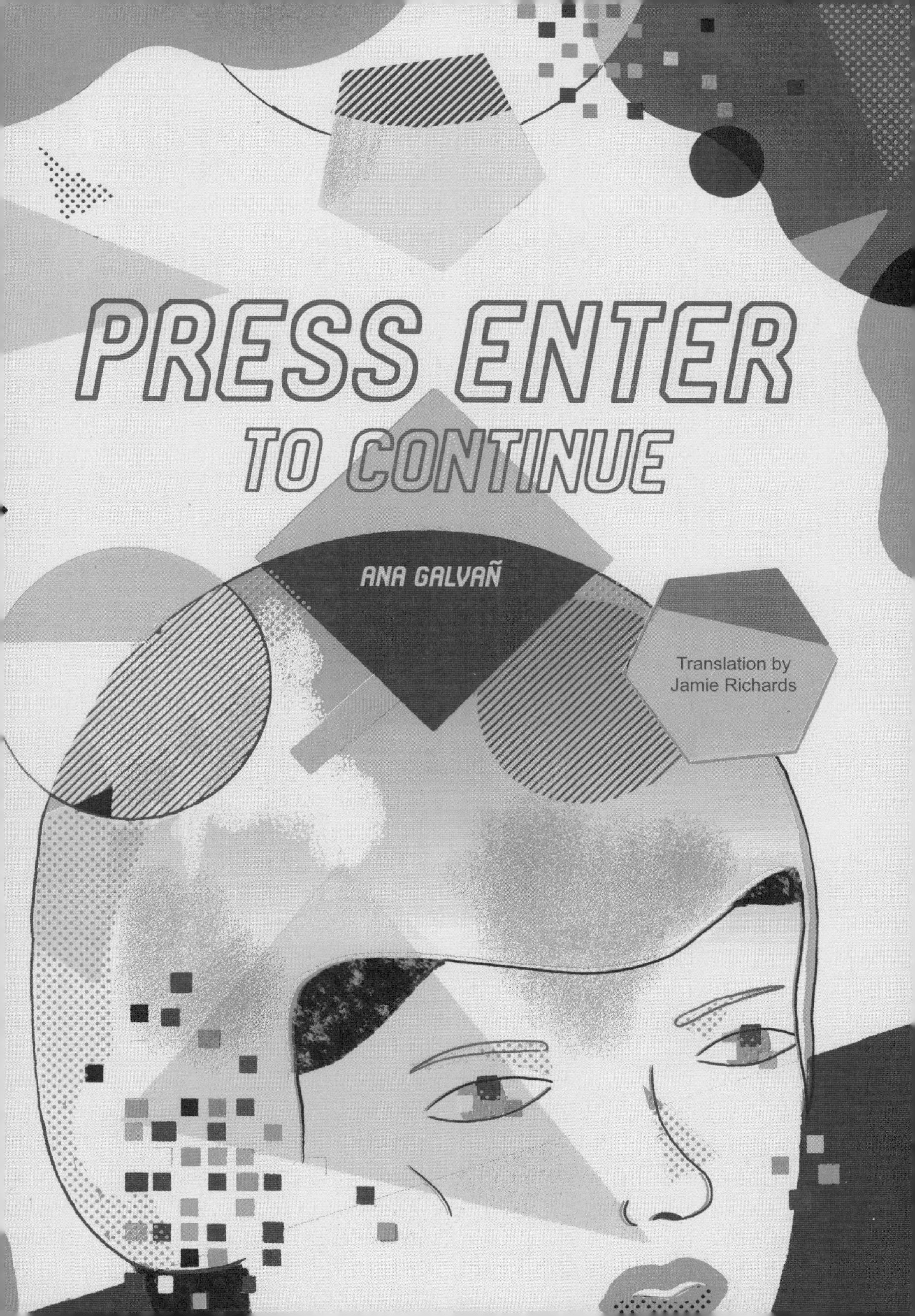
PRESS ENTER
TO CONTINUE
ANA GALVAÑ
Translation by
Jamie Richards

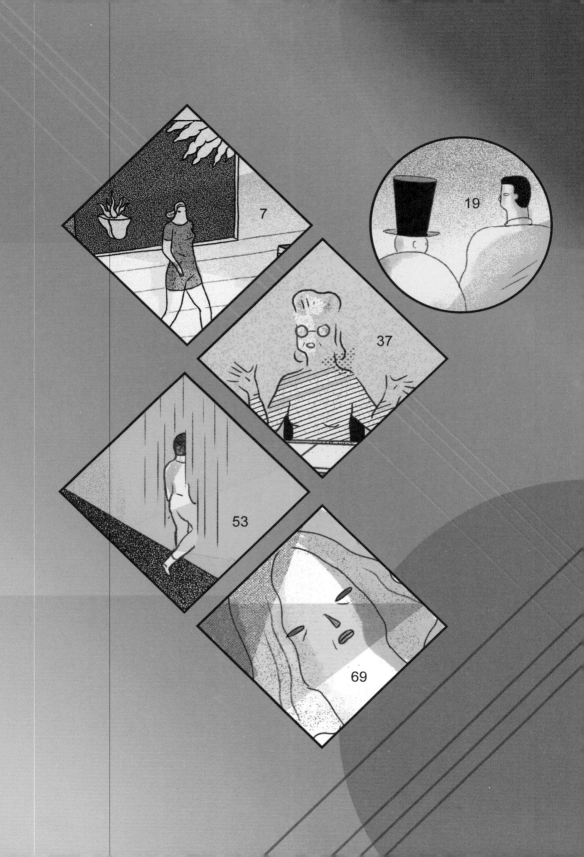

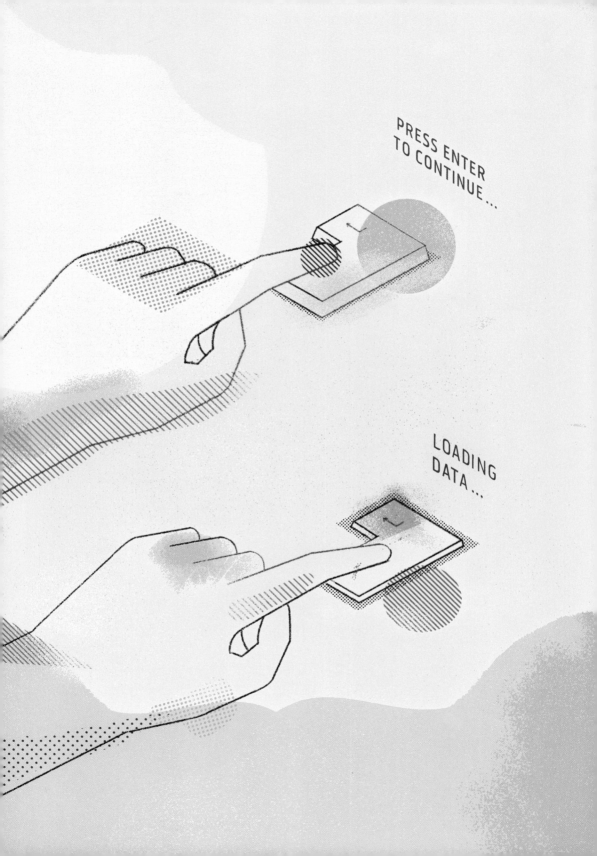

PRESS ENTER
TO CONTINUE...

LOADING
DATA...

FANTAGRAPHICS
BOOKS INC.
7563 Lake City Way NE
Seattle, Washington, 98115
www.fantagraphics.com

Translated from Spanish by Jamie Richards
Editor and Associate Publisher: Eric Reynolds
Book Design: Ana Galvañ • Production: Paul Baresh and
Keeli McCarthy • Proofreading: RJ Casey • Publisher: Gary Groth

ISBN 978-1-68396-216-8
Library of Congress Control Number:
2018967021

First printing:
July 2019
Printed in
China

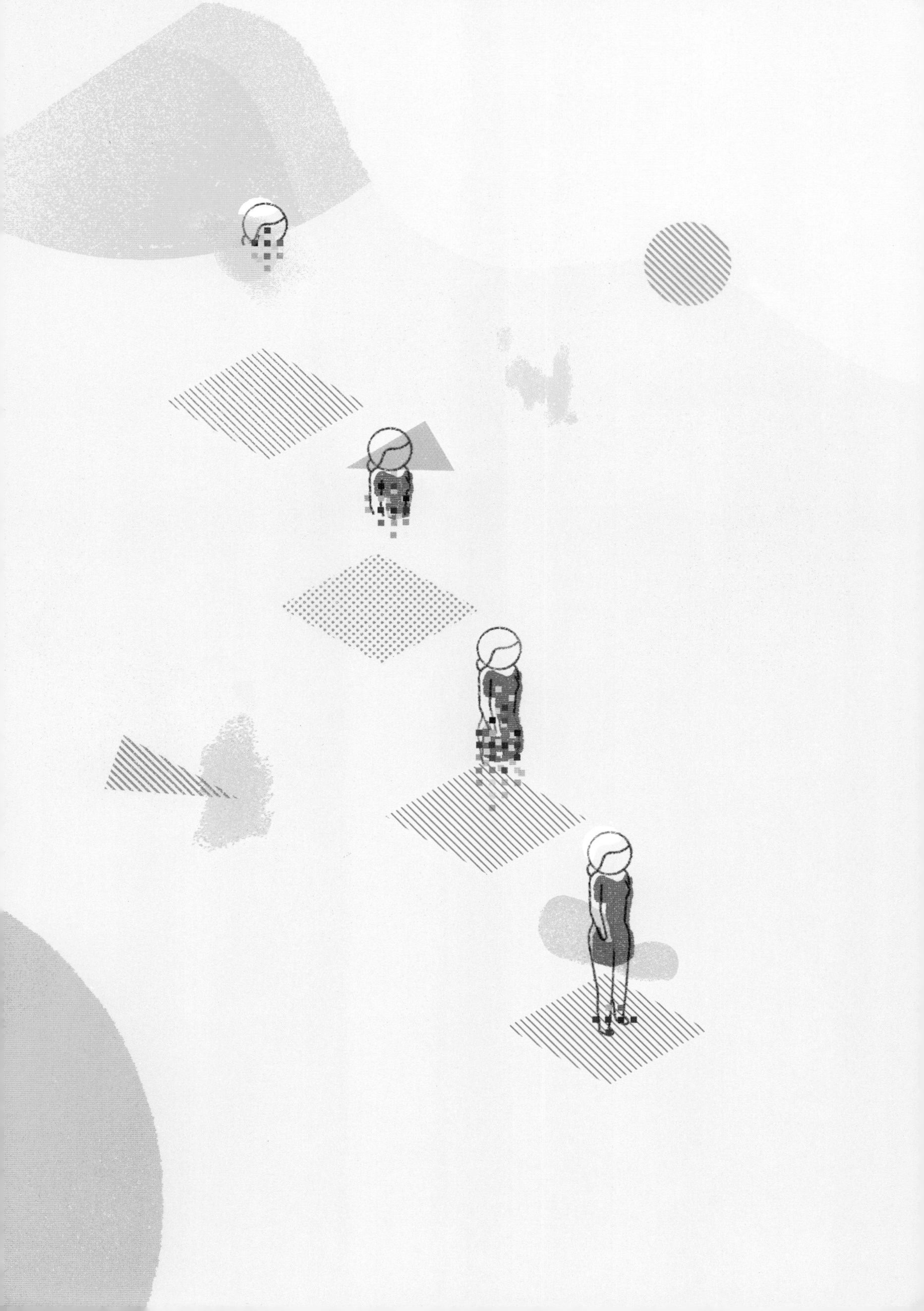

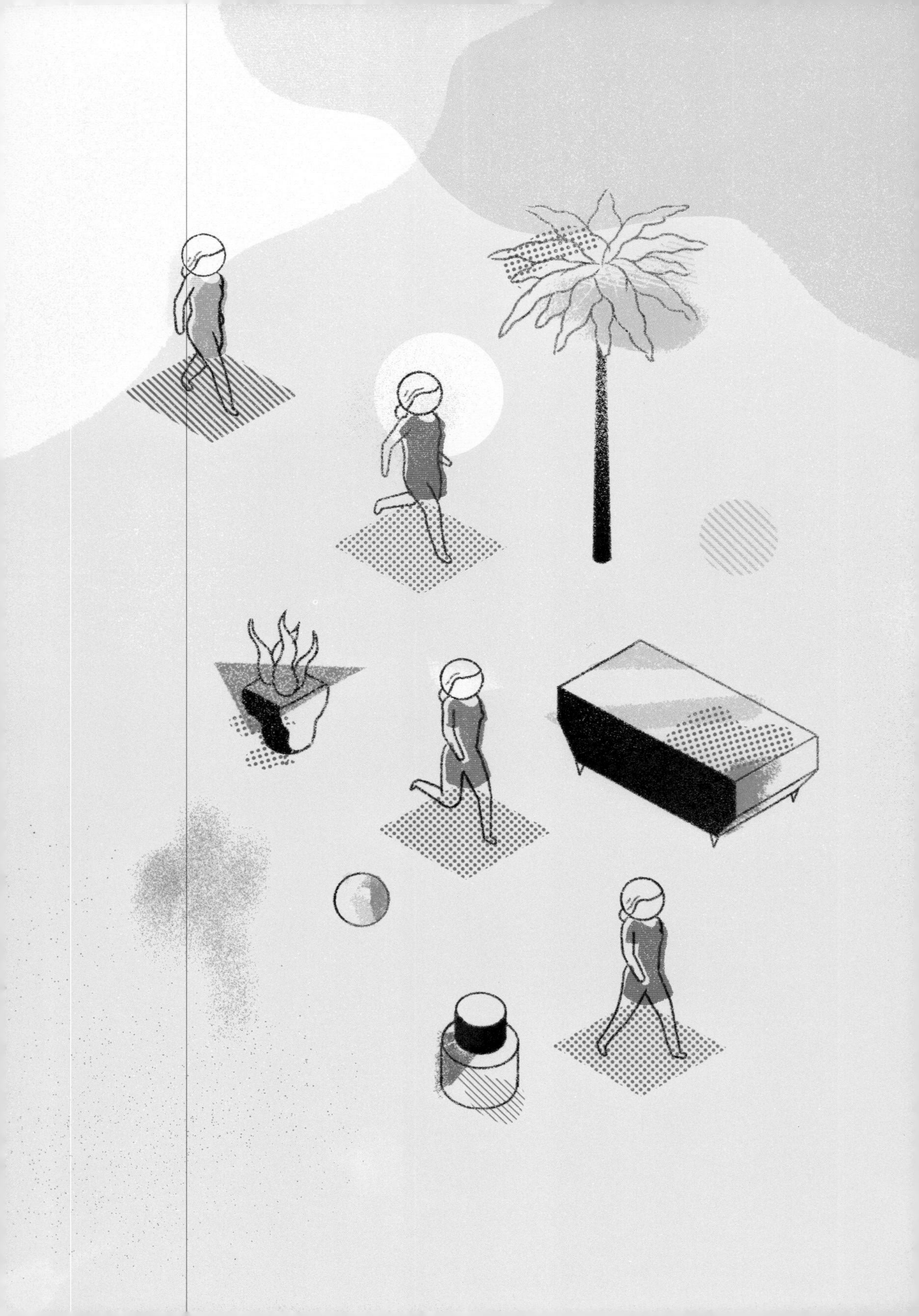

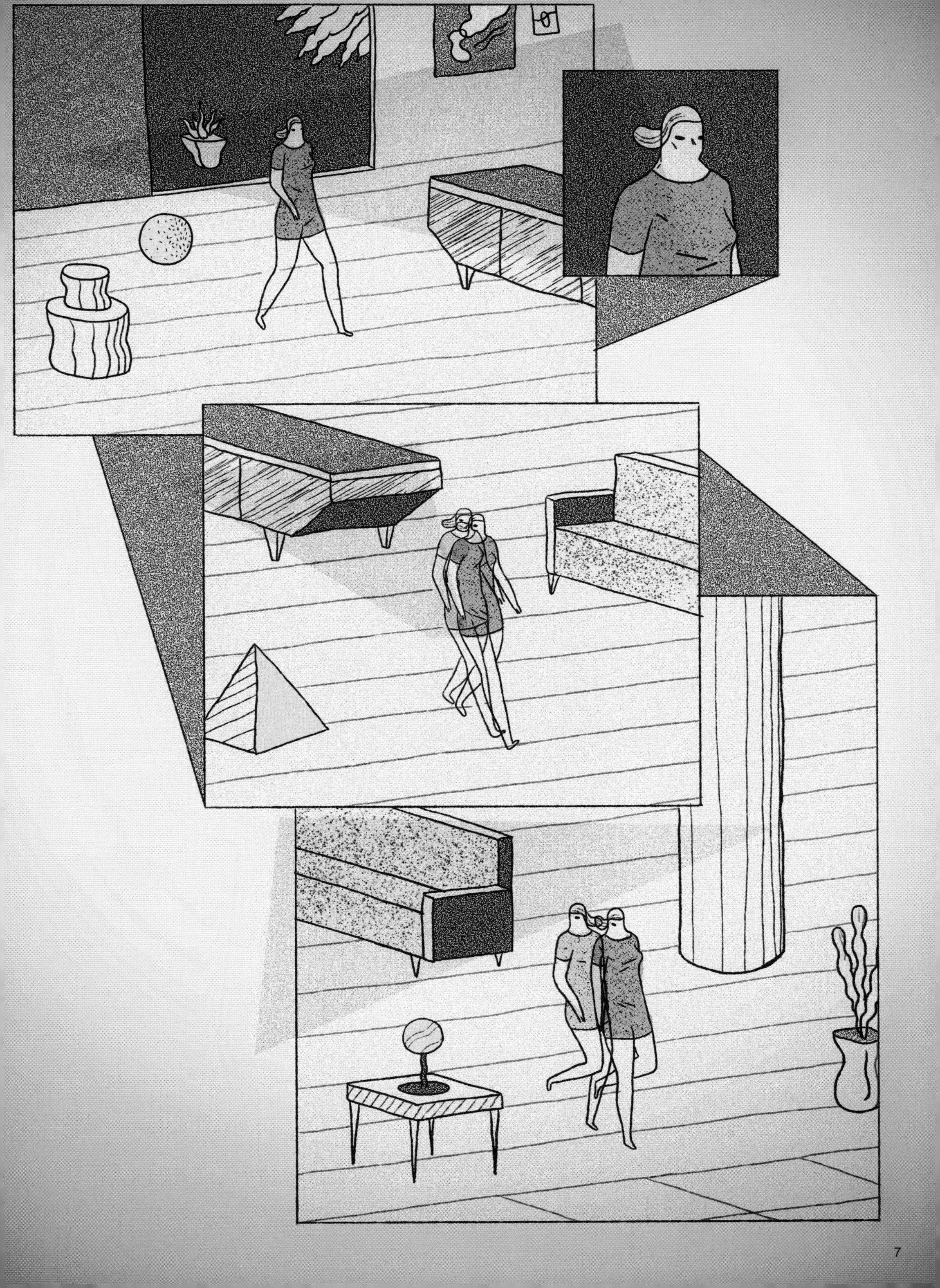

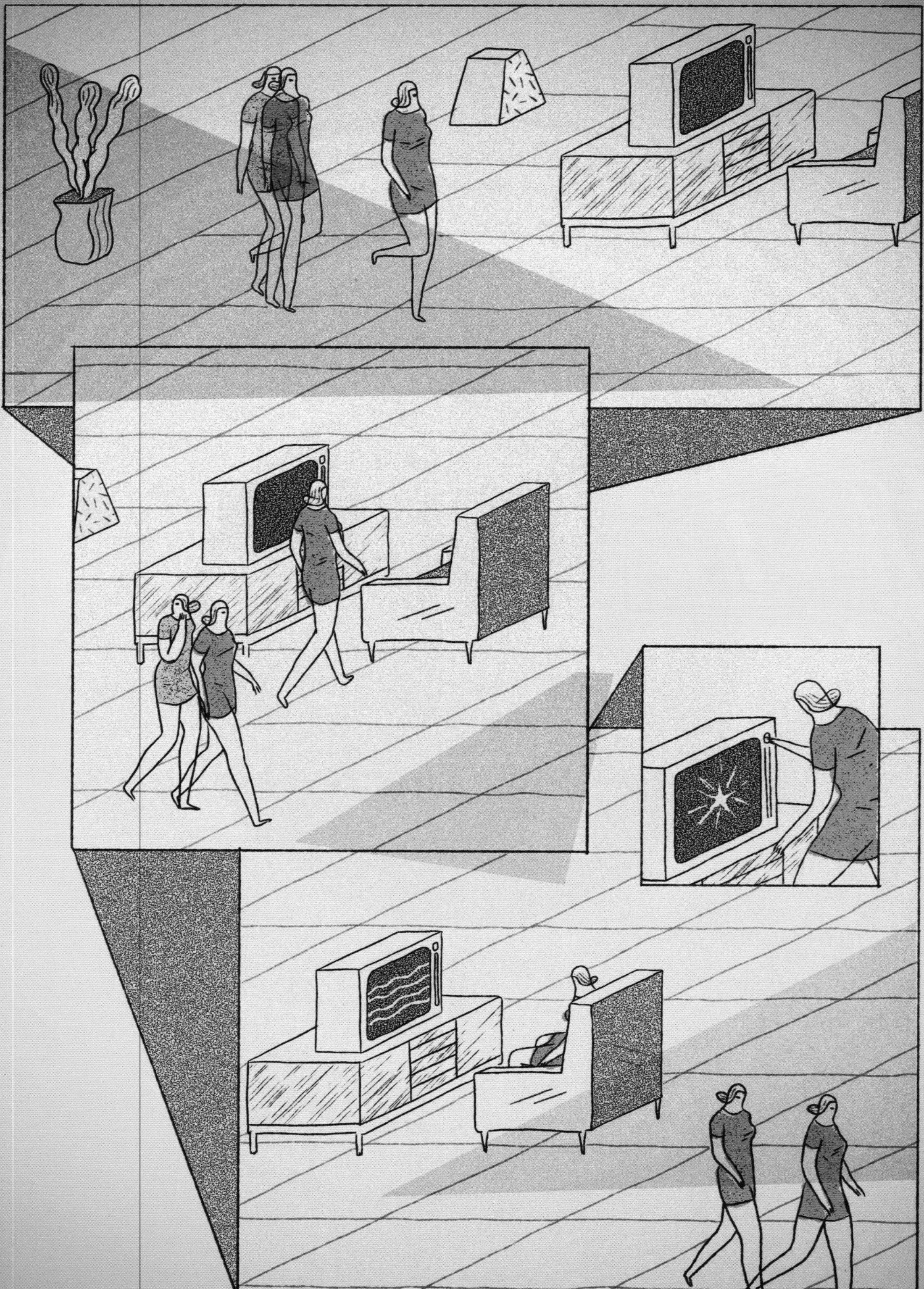

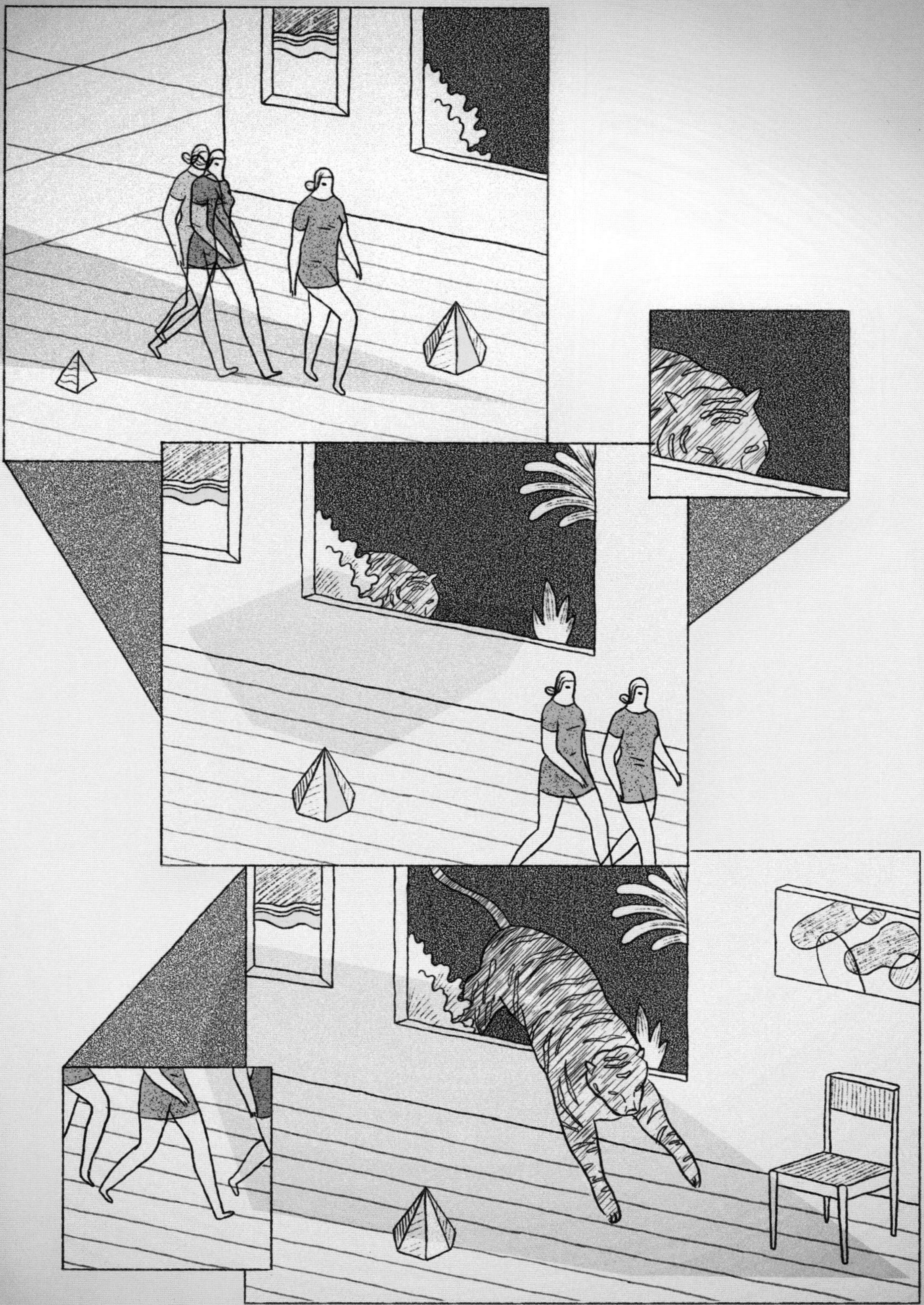

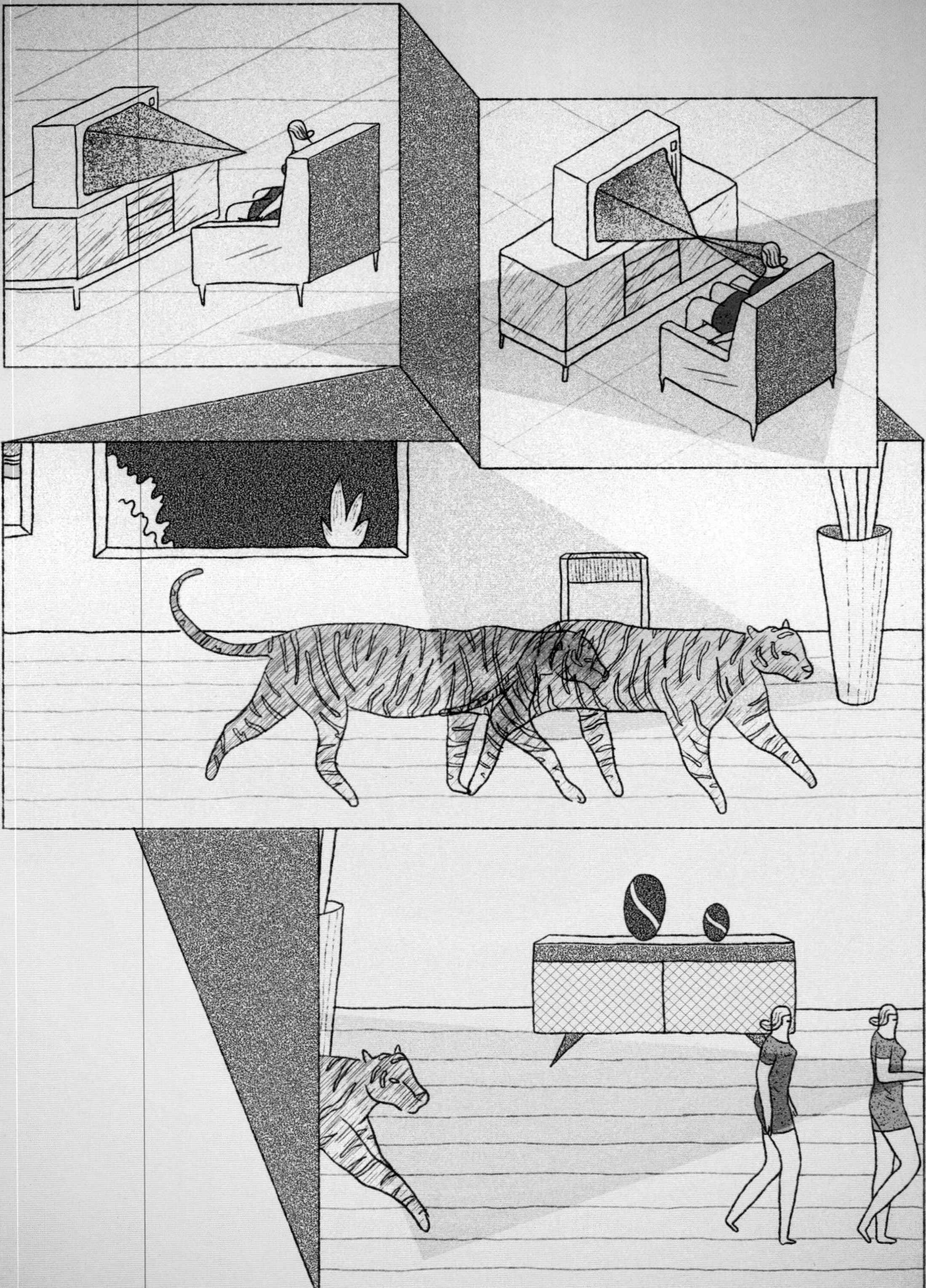

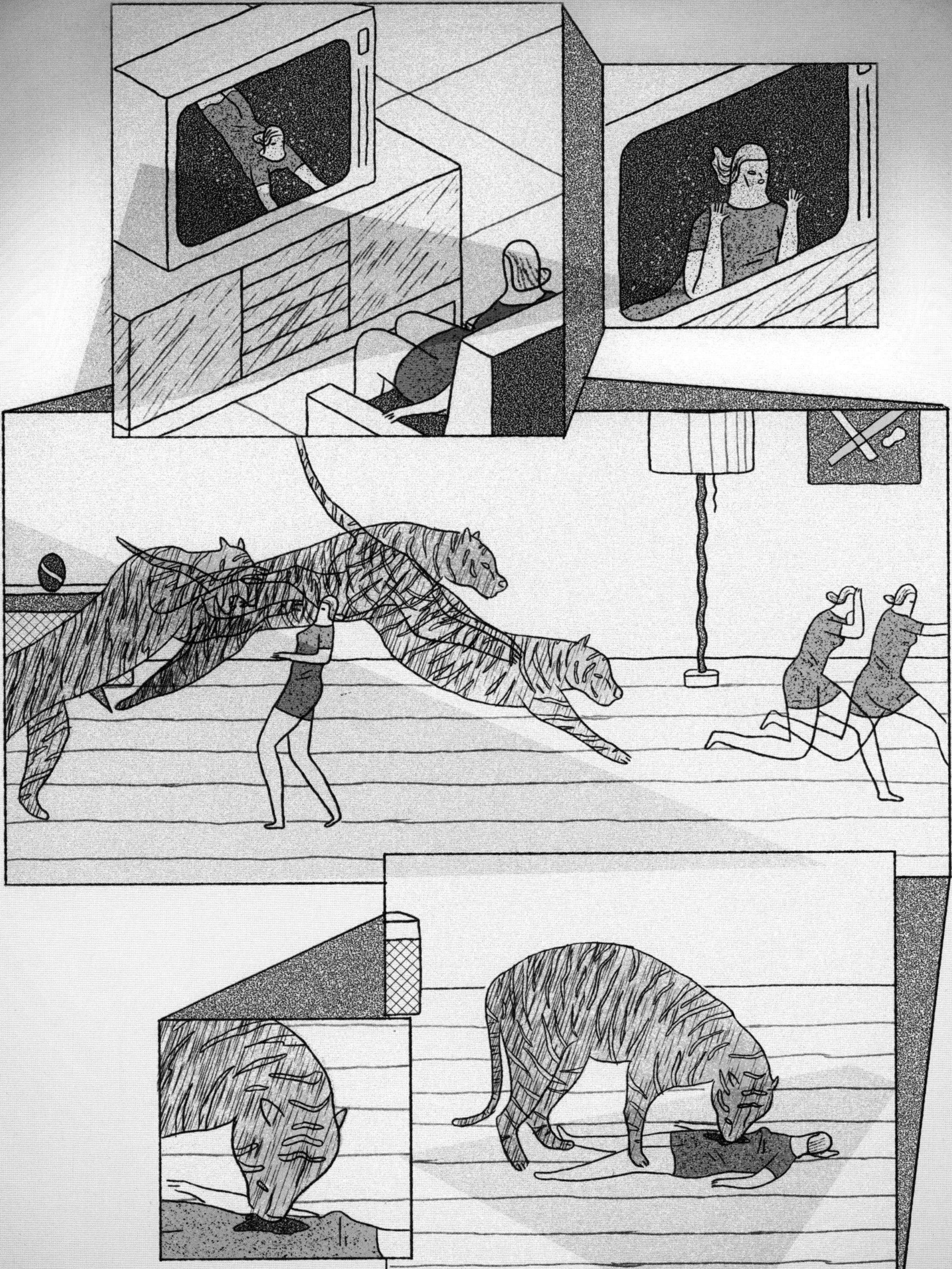

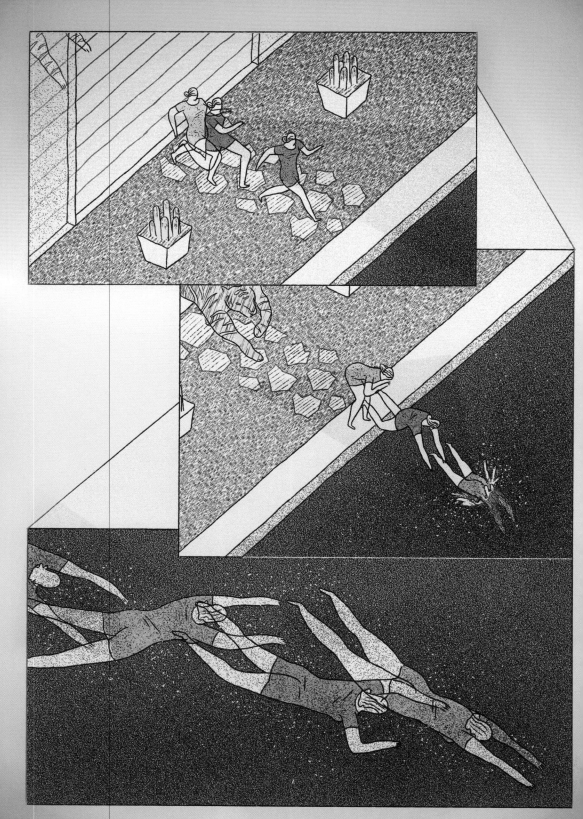

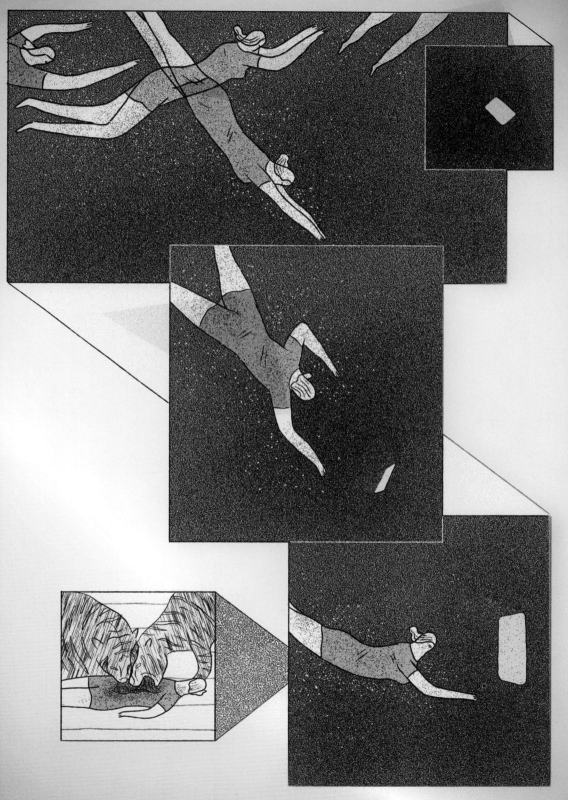

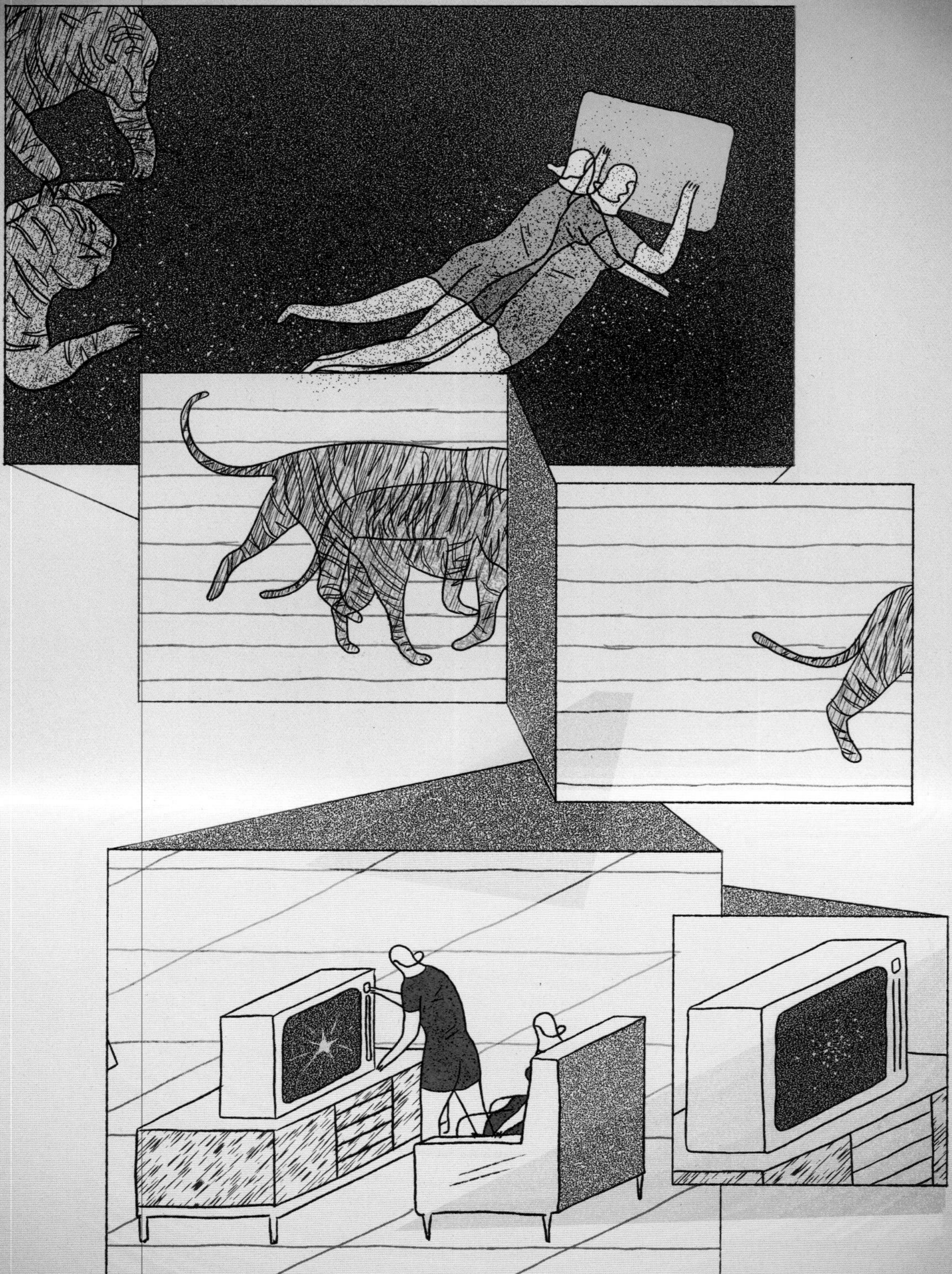

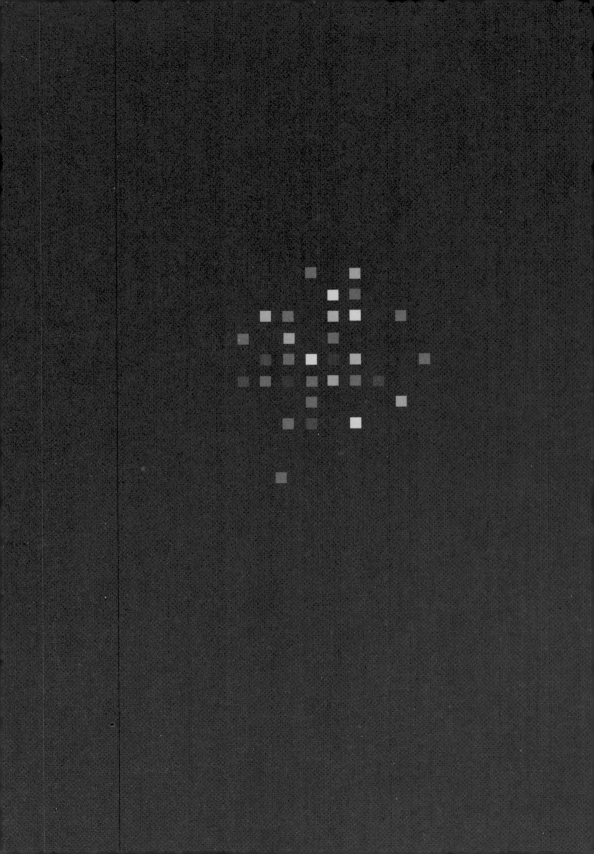

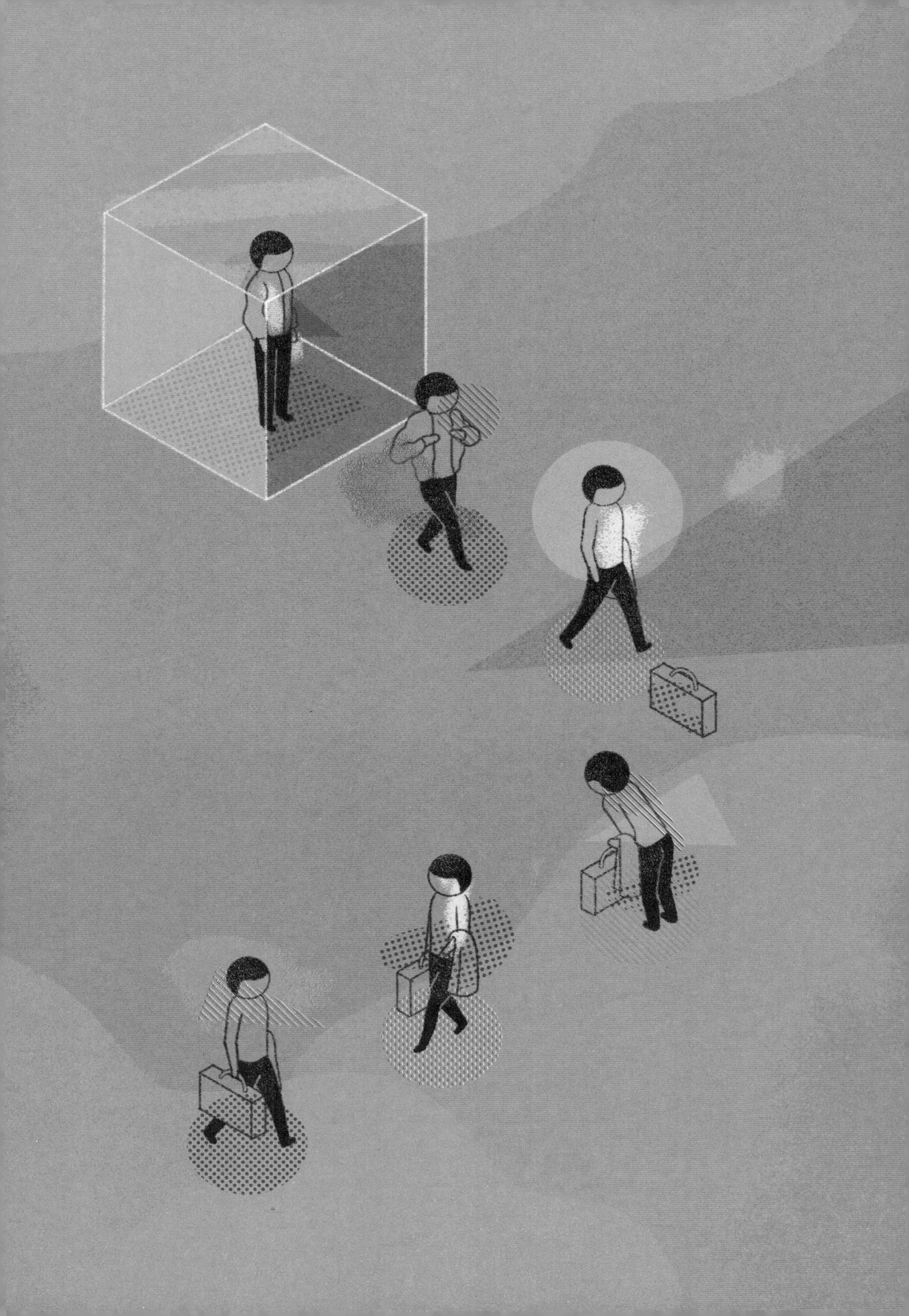

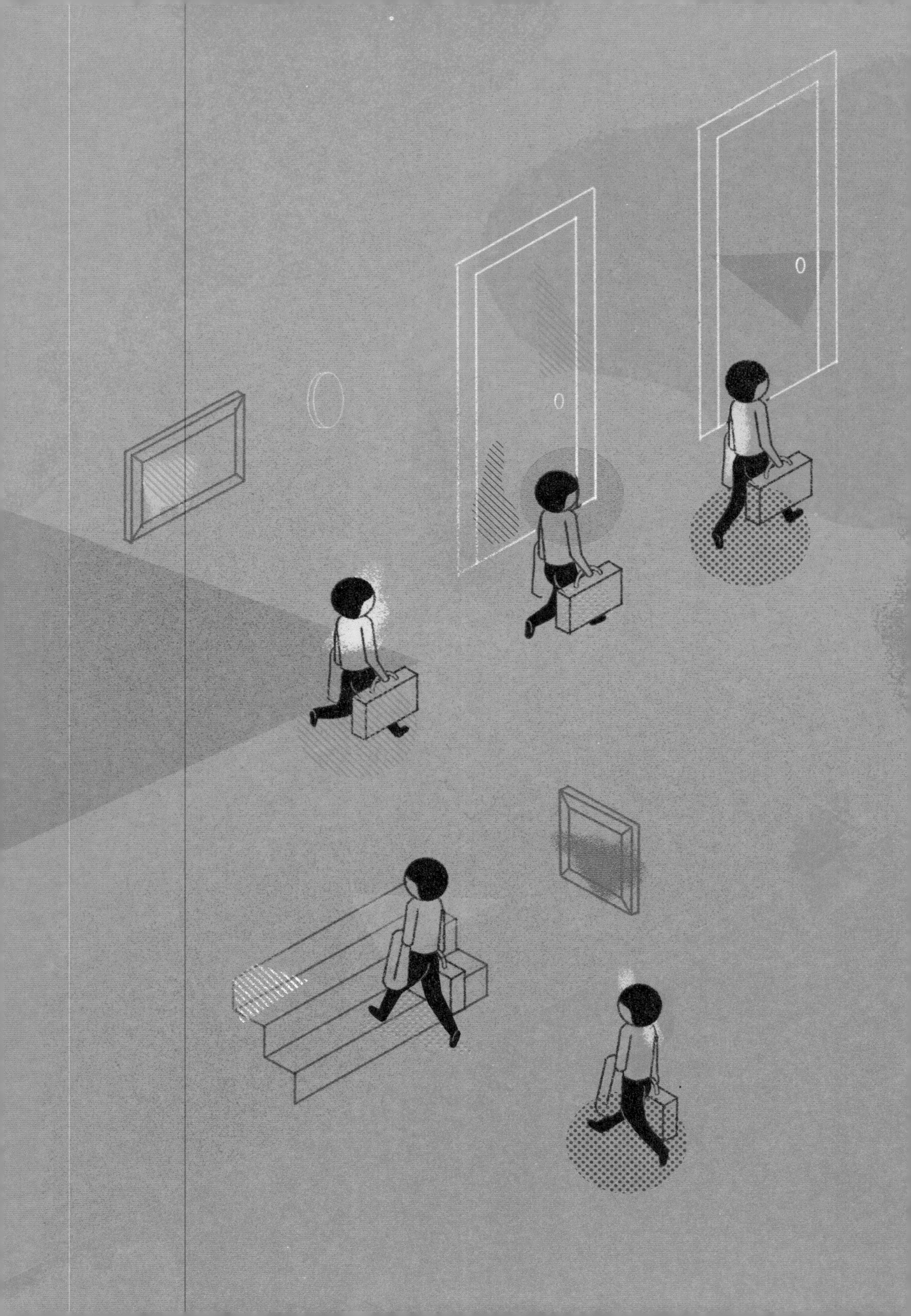

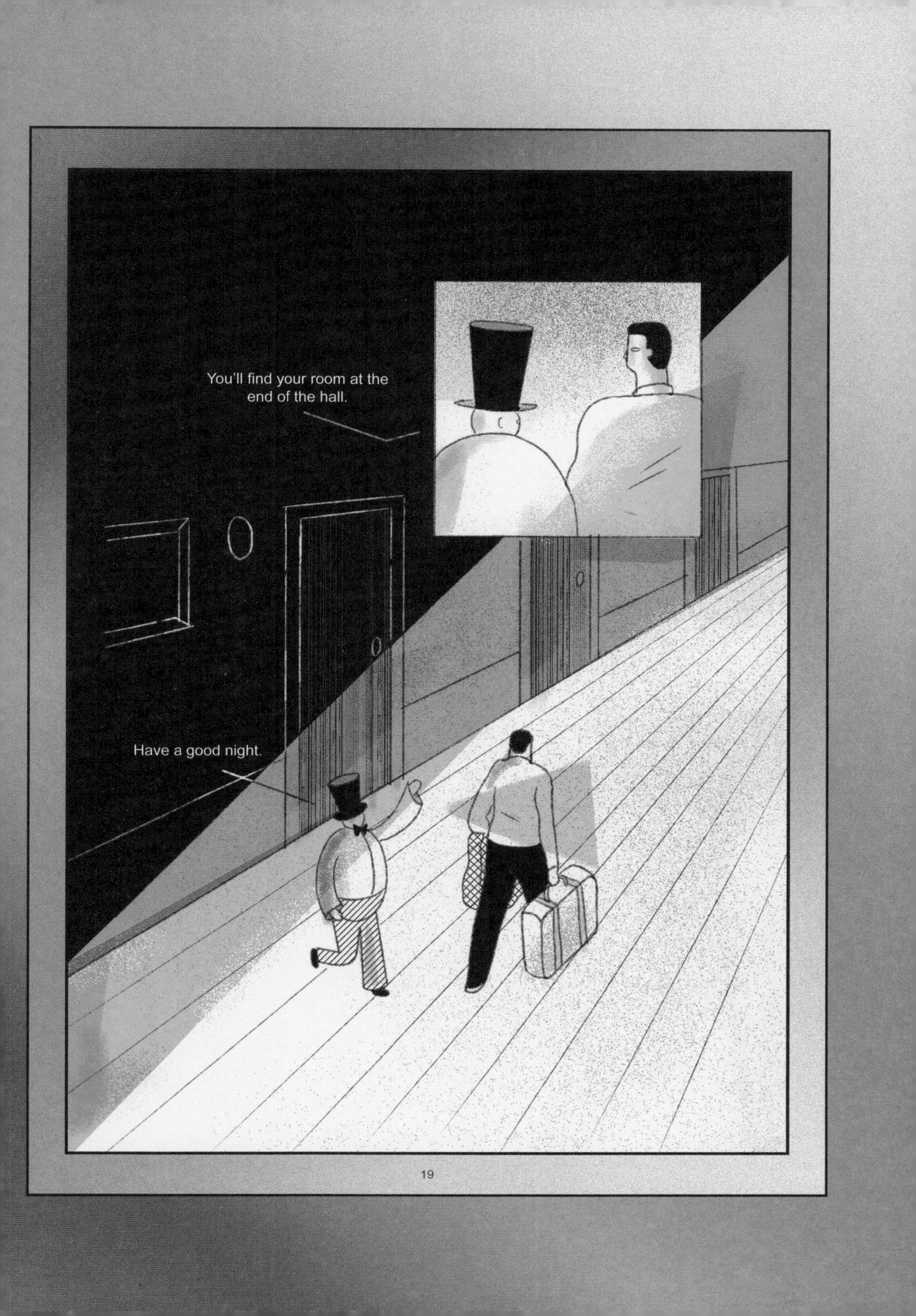
You'll find your room at the end of the hall.
Have a good night.

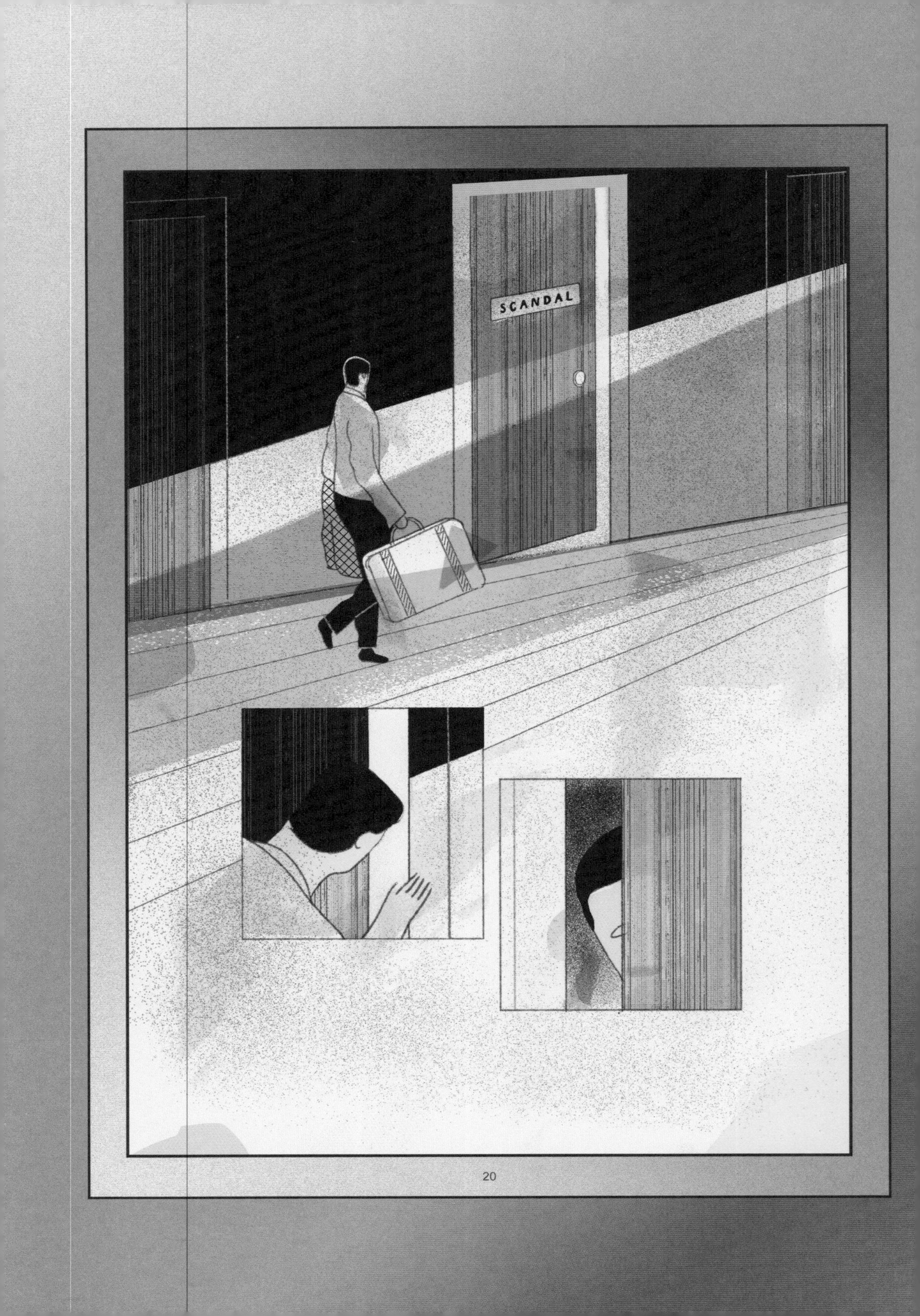
SCANDAL

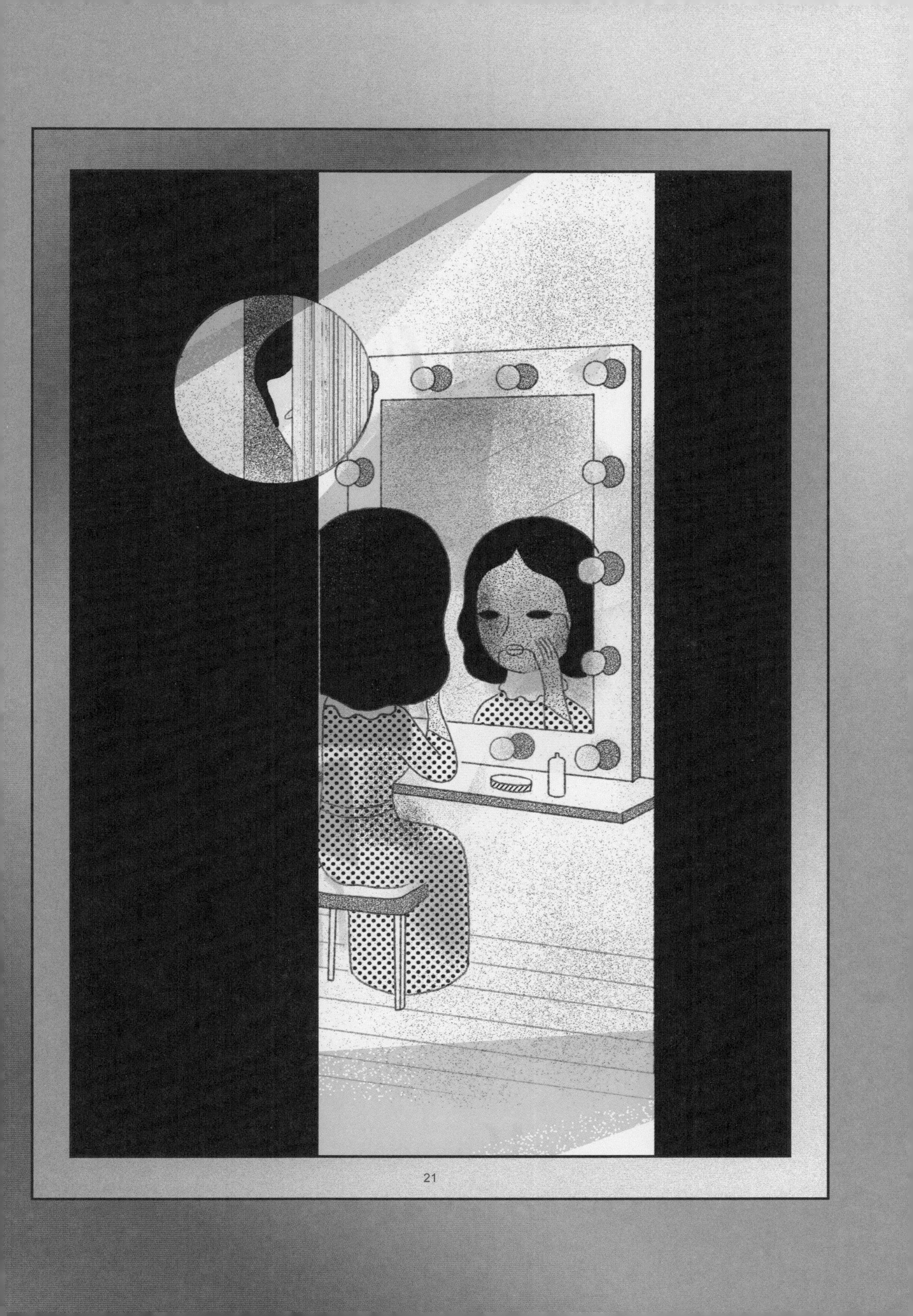

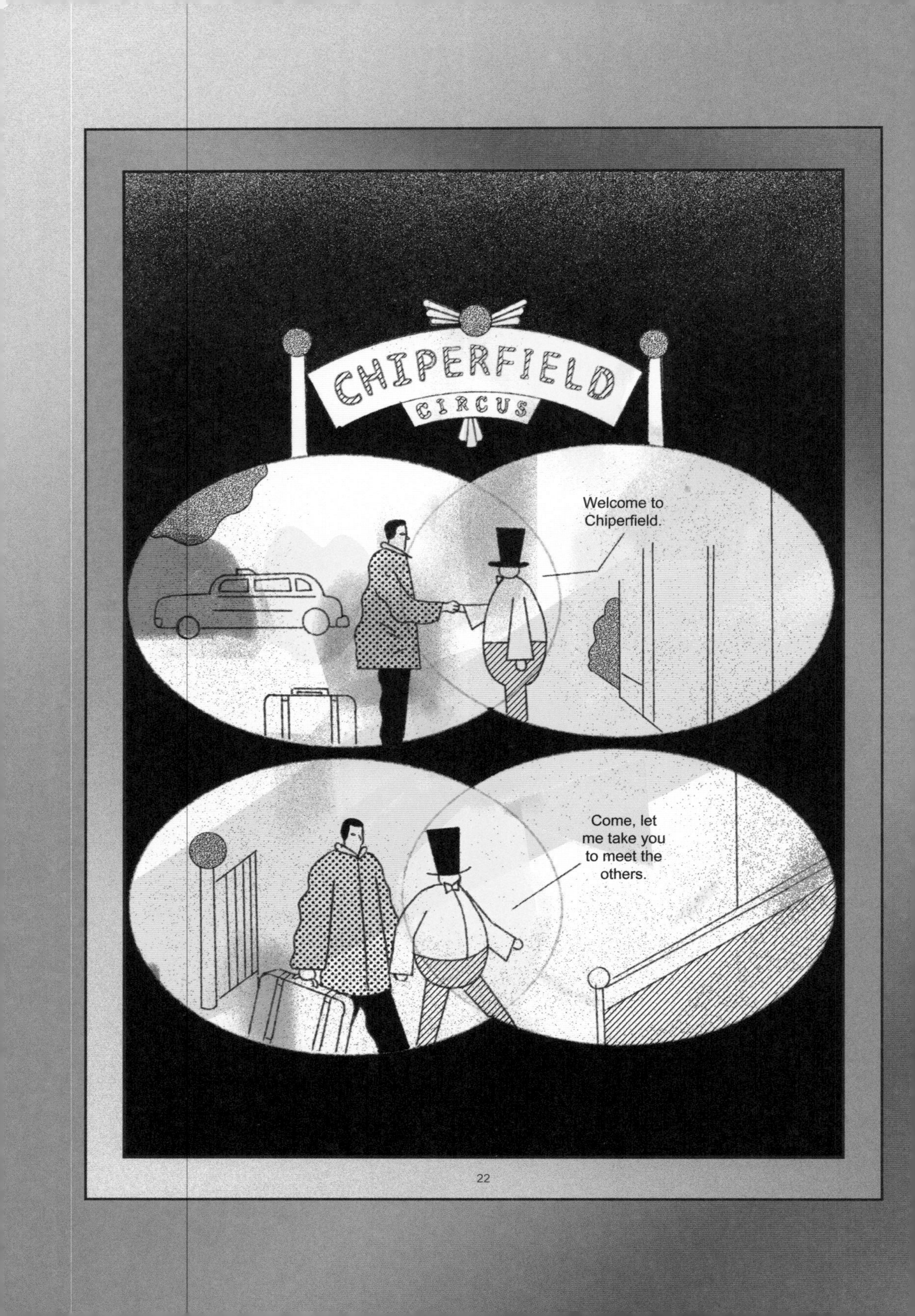
CHIPERFIELD
CIRCUS
Welcome to Chiperfield.
Come, let me take you to meet the others.

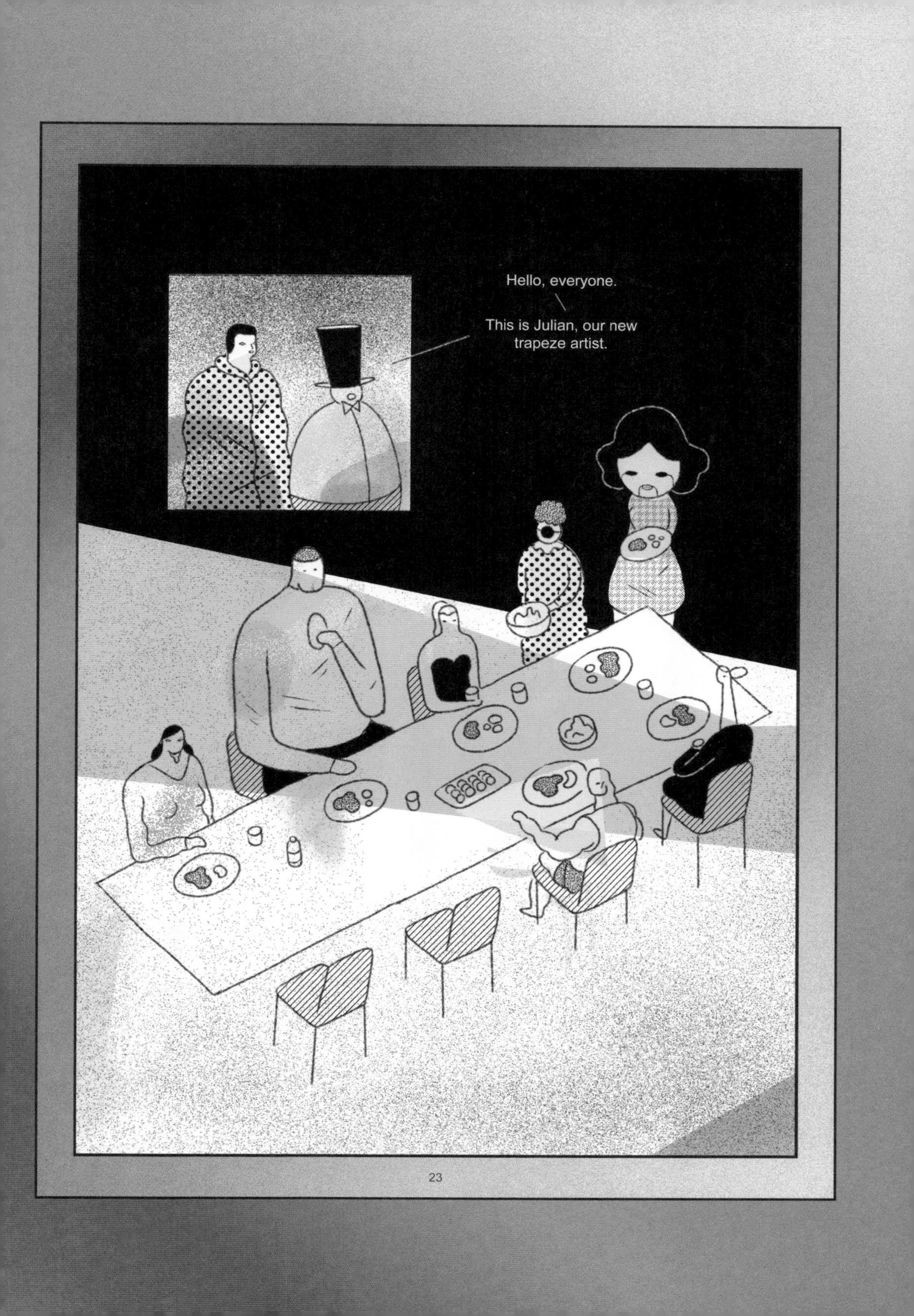
Hello, everyone.
This is Julian, our new trapeze artist.

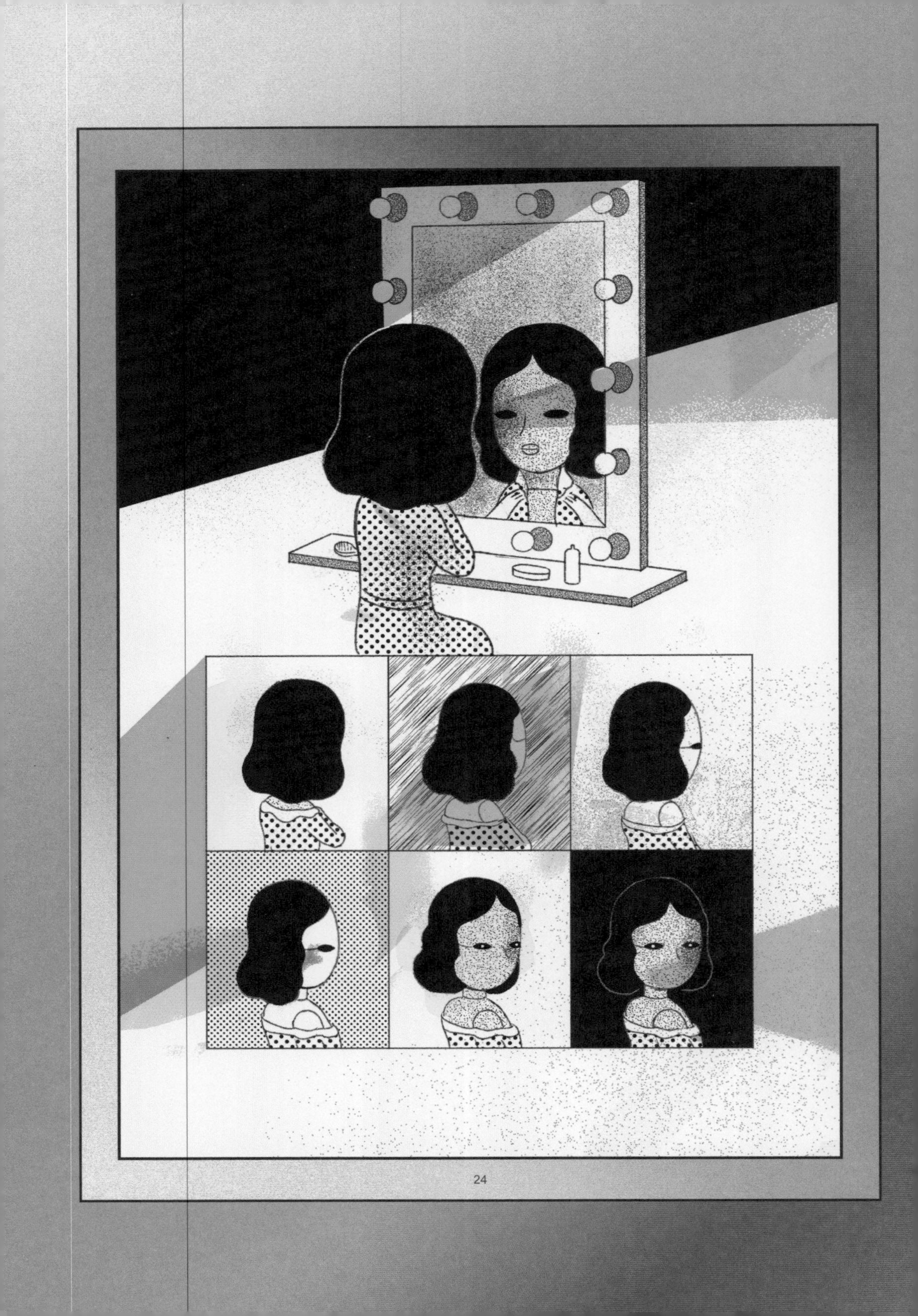

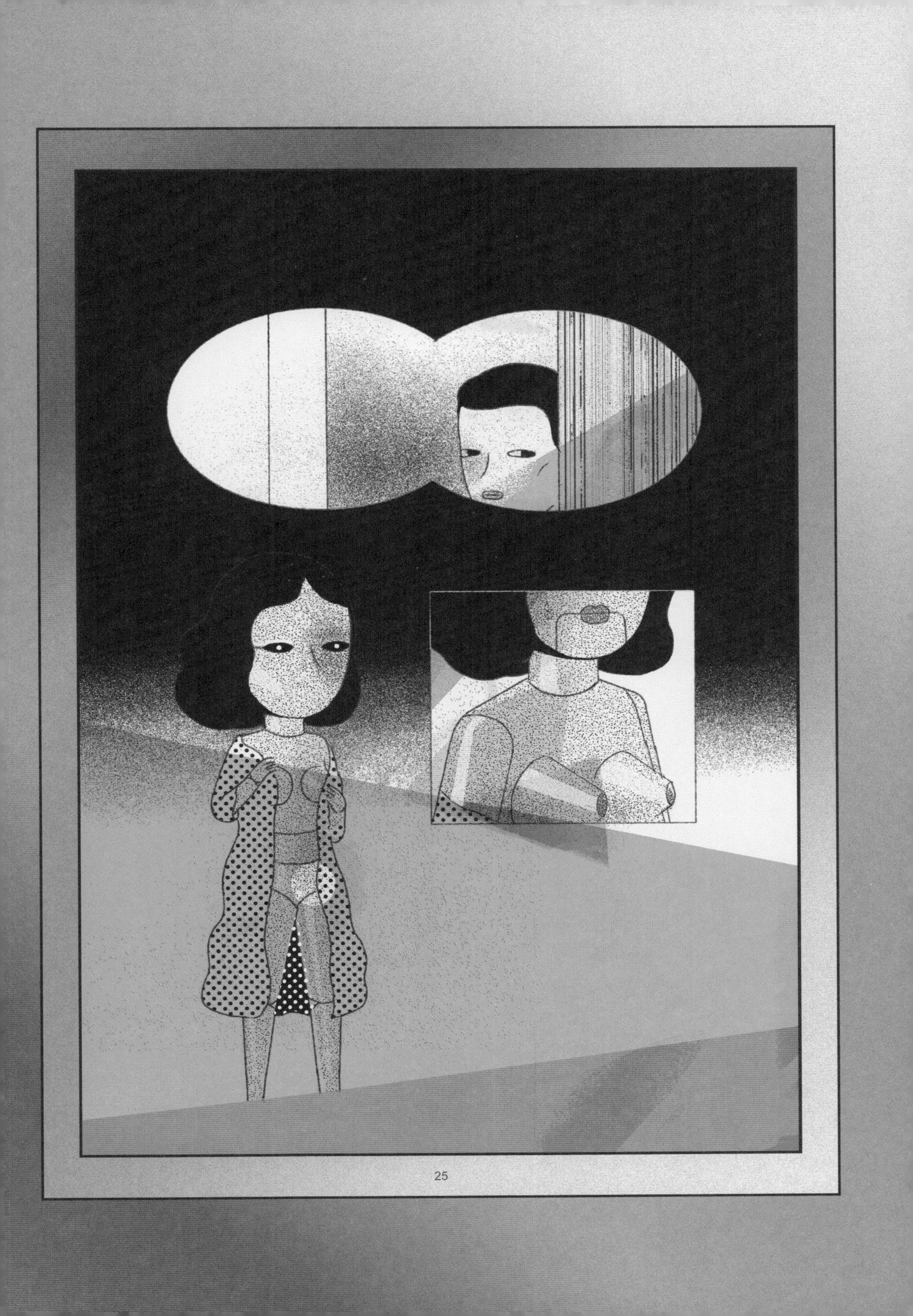

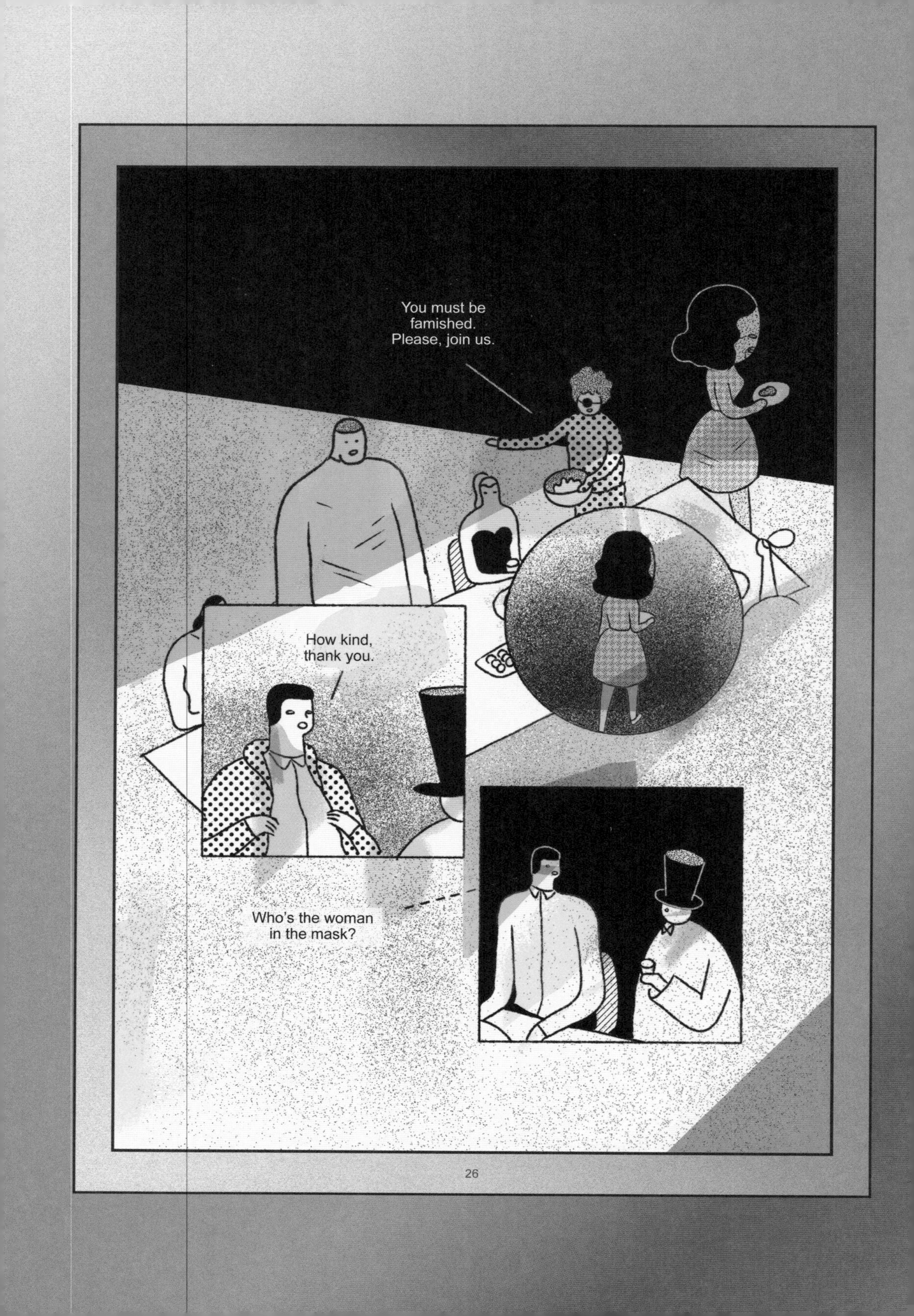
You must be famished. Please, join us.
How kind, thank you.
Who's the woman in the mask?

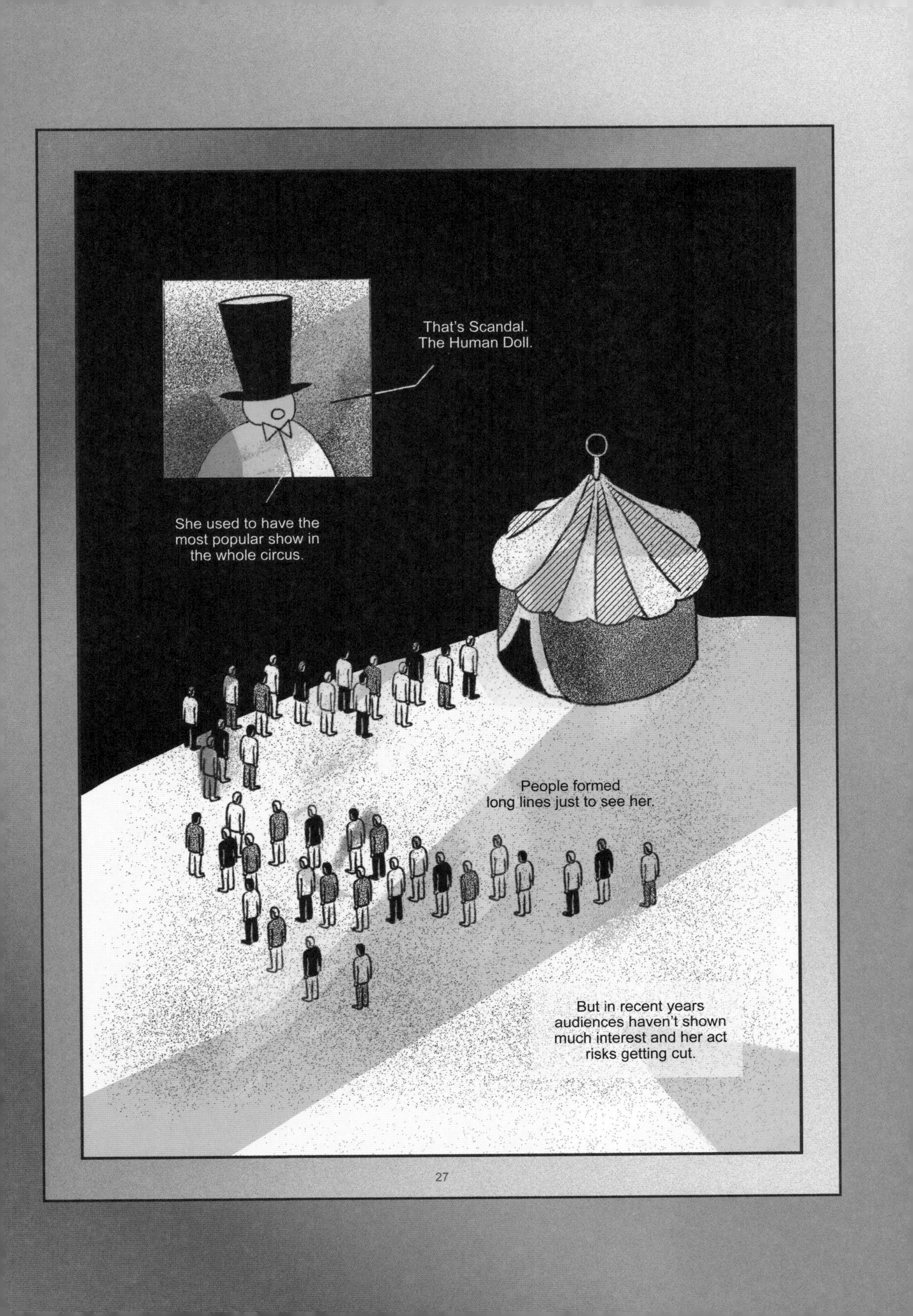
That's Scandal.
The Human Doll.
She used to have the most popular show in the whole circus.
People formed long lines just to see her.
But in recent years audiences haven't shown much interest and her act risks getting cut.

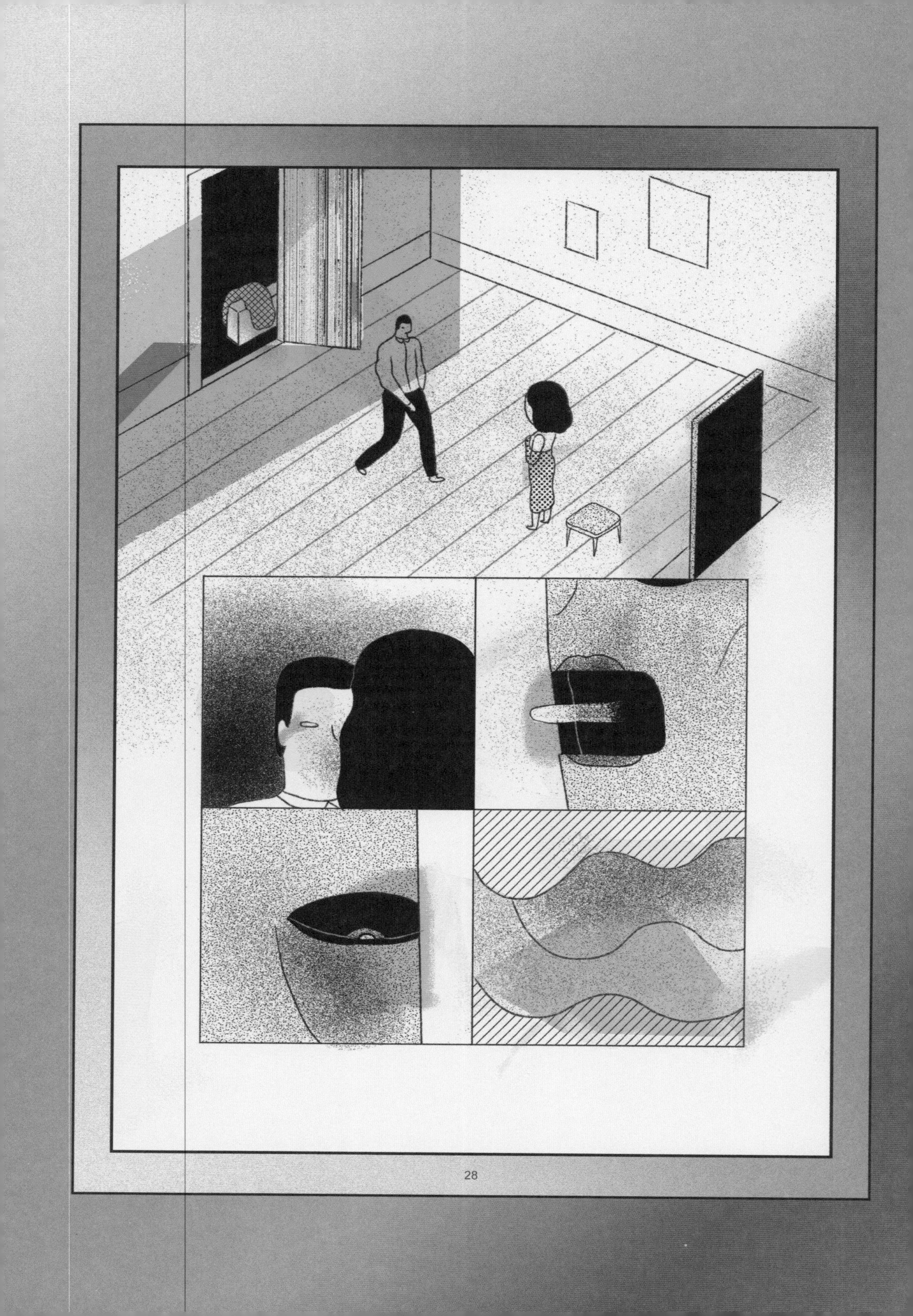

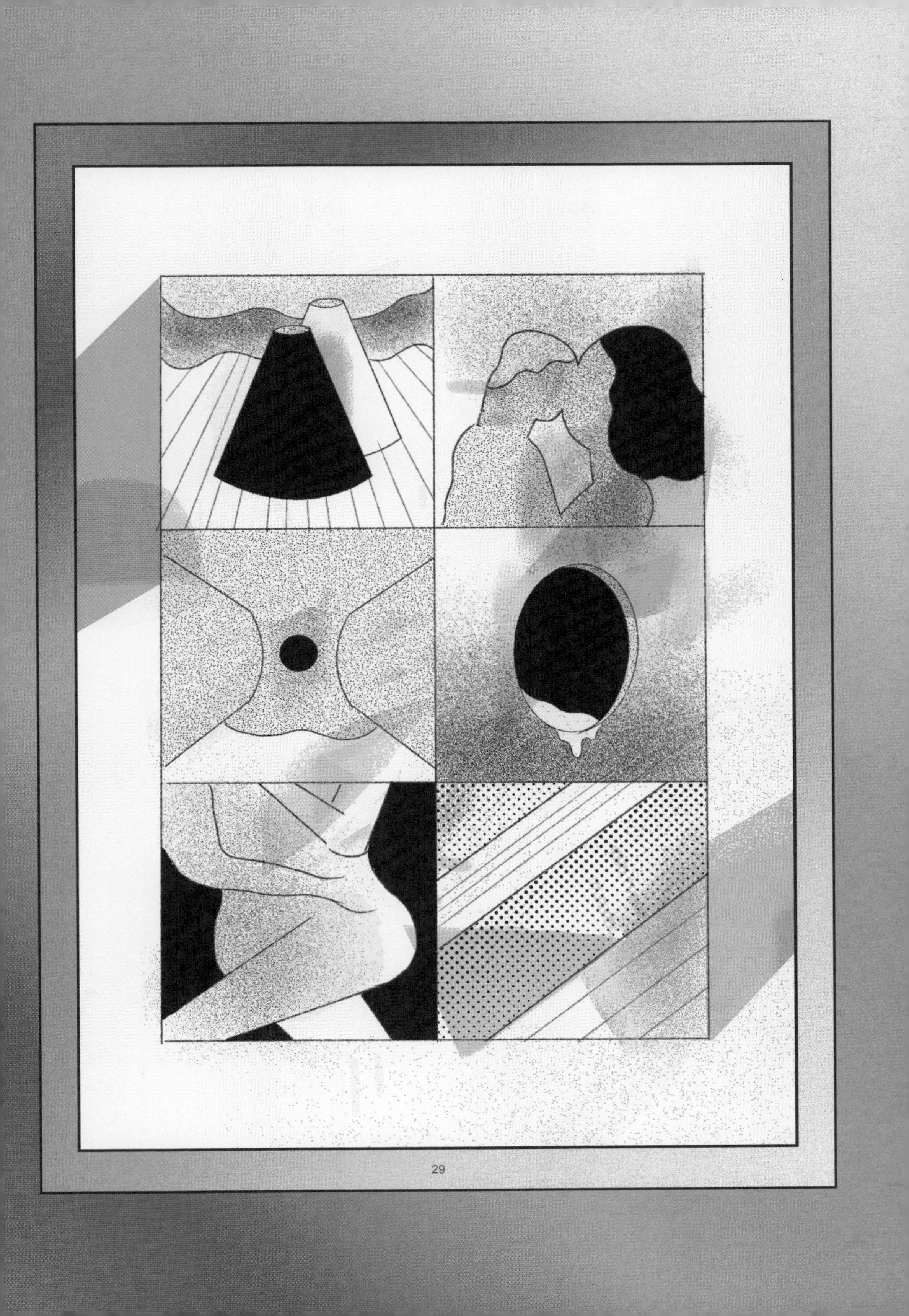

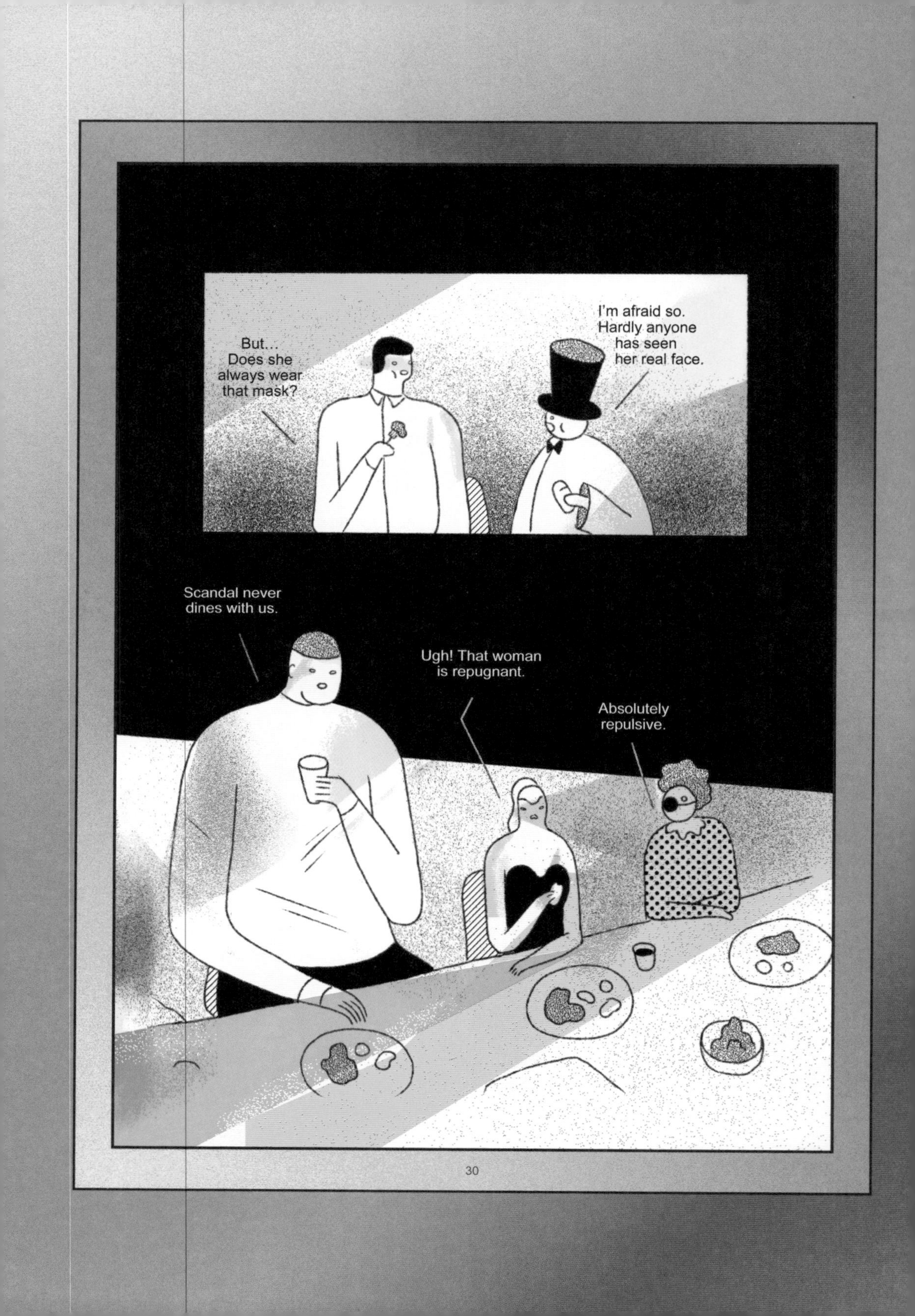
But... Does she always wear that mask?
I'm afraid so. Hardly anyone has seen her real face.
Scandal never dines with us.
Ugh! That woman is repugnant.
Absolutely repulsive.

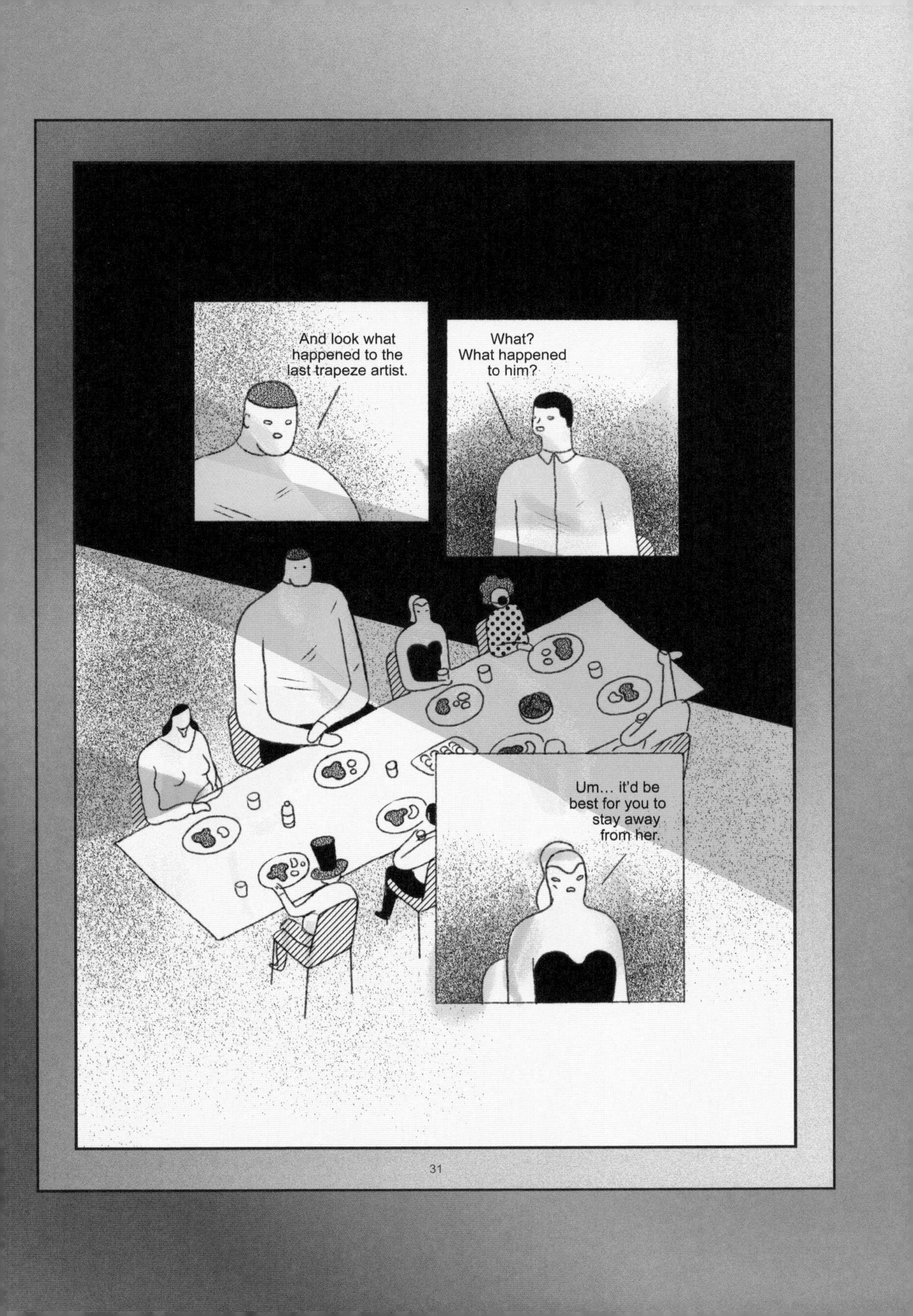
And look what happened to the last trapeze artist.
What? What happened to him?
Um… it'd be best for you to stay away from her.

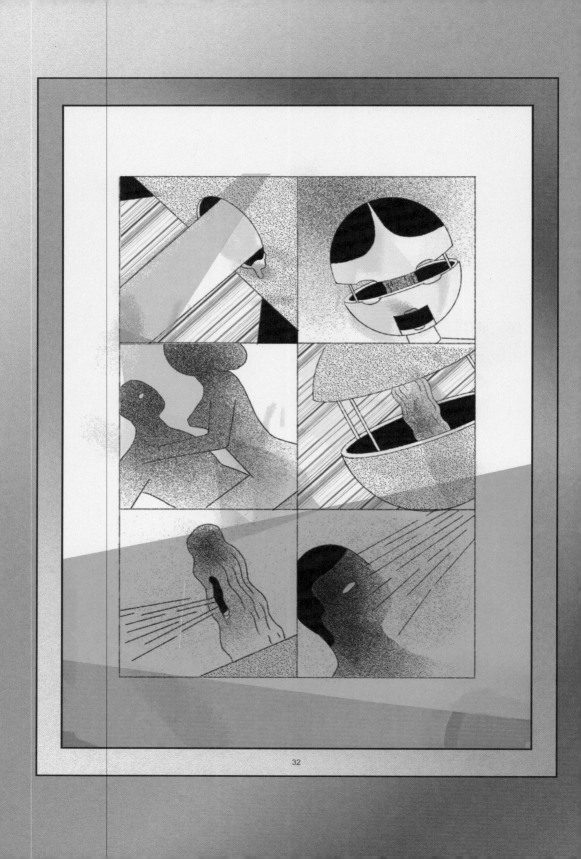

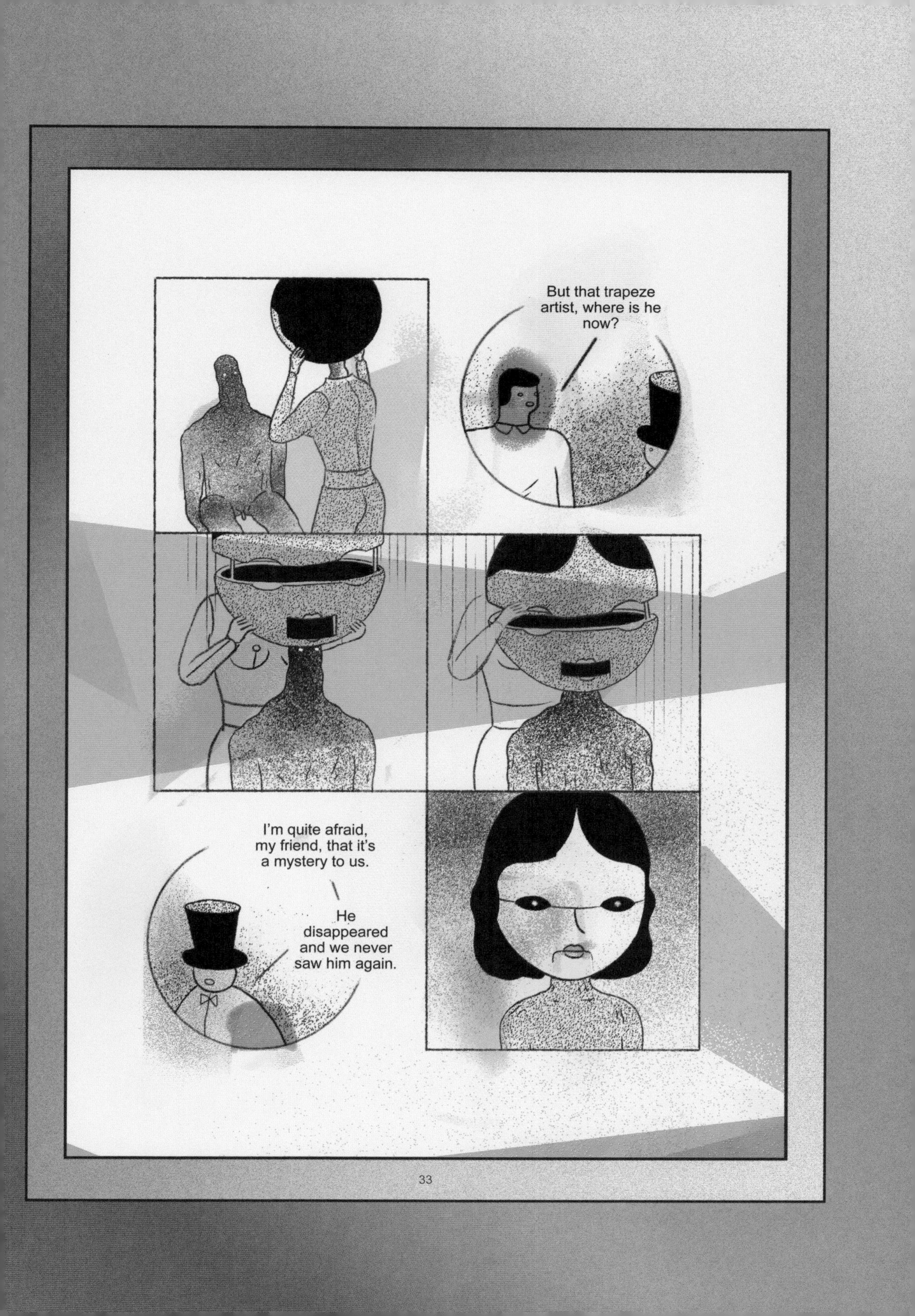
But that trapeze artist, where is he now?
I'm quite afraid, my friend, that it's a mystery to us.
He disappeared and we never saw him again.

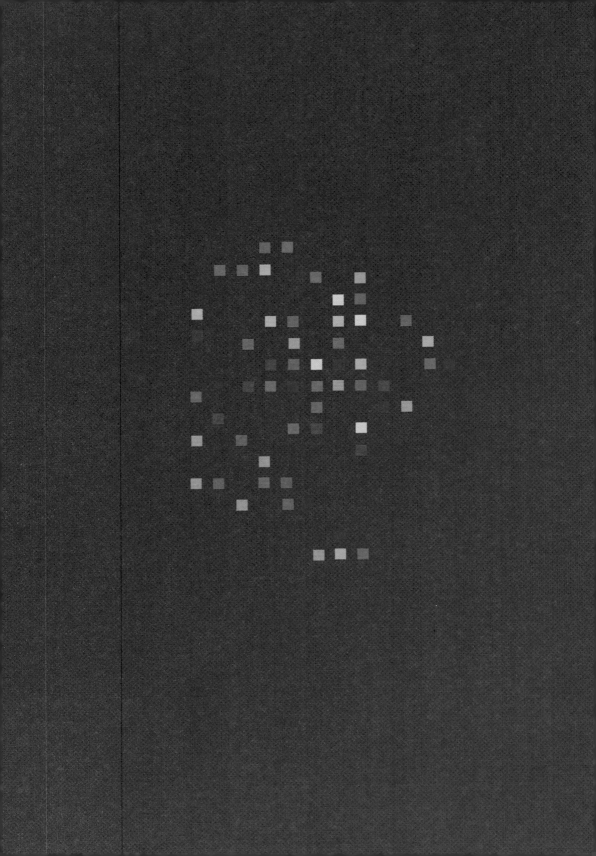

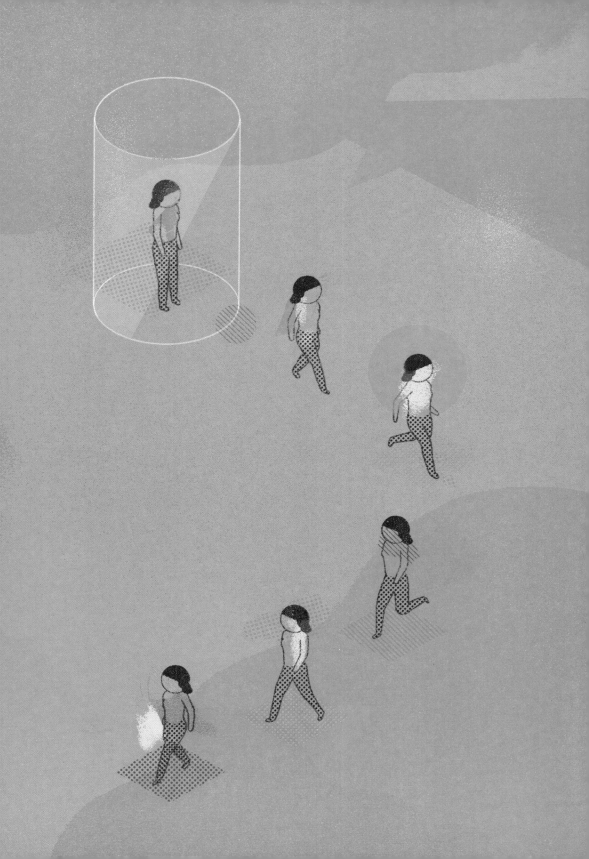

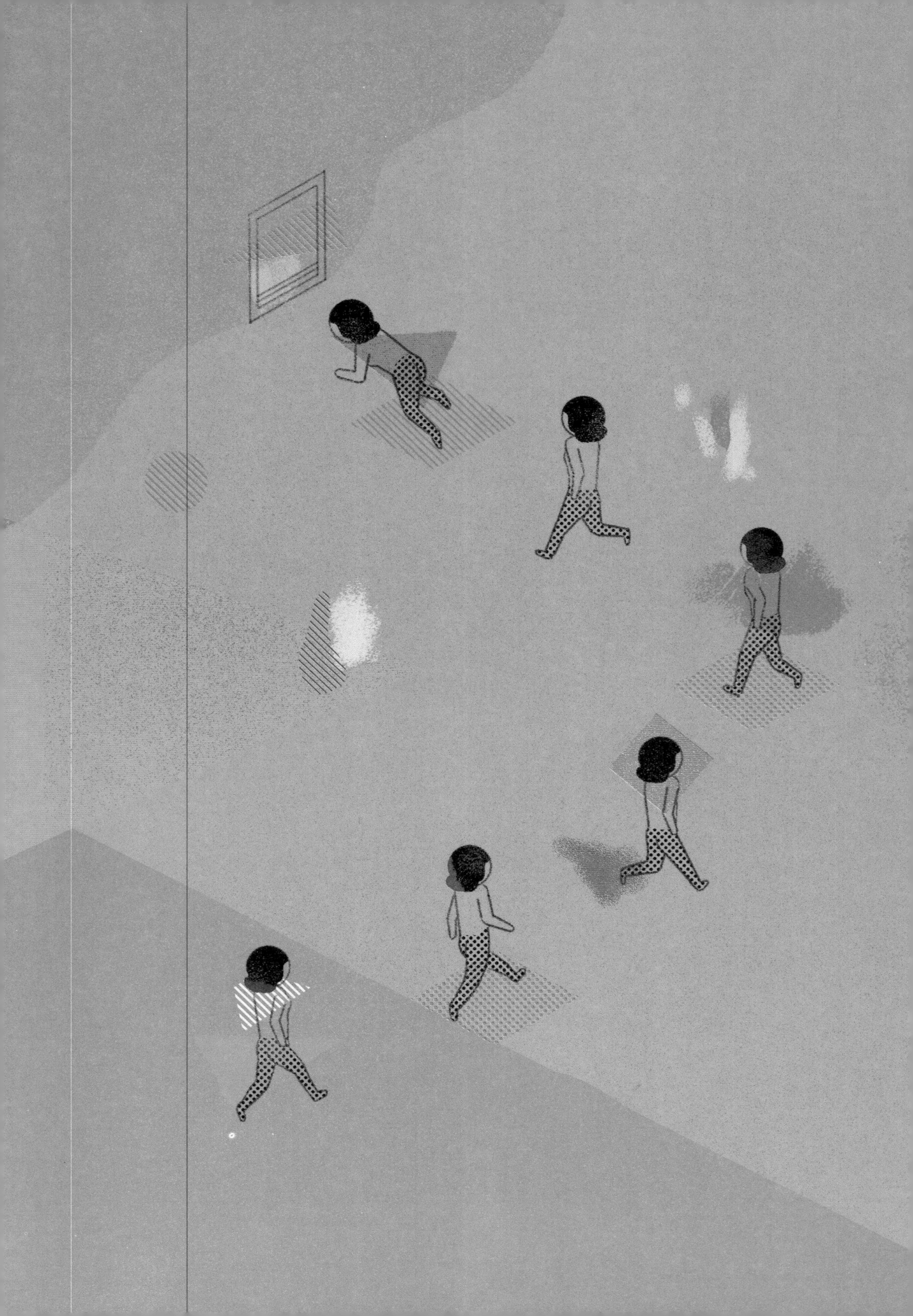

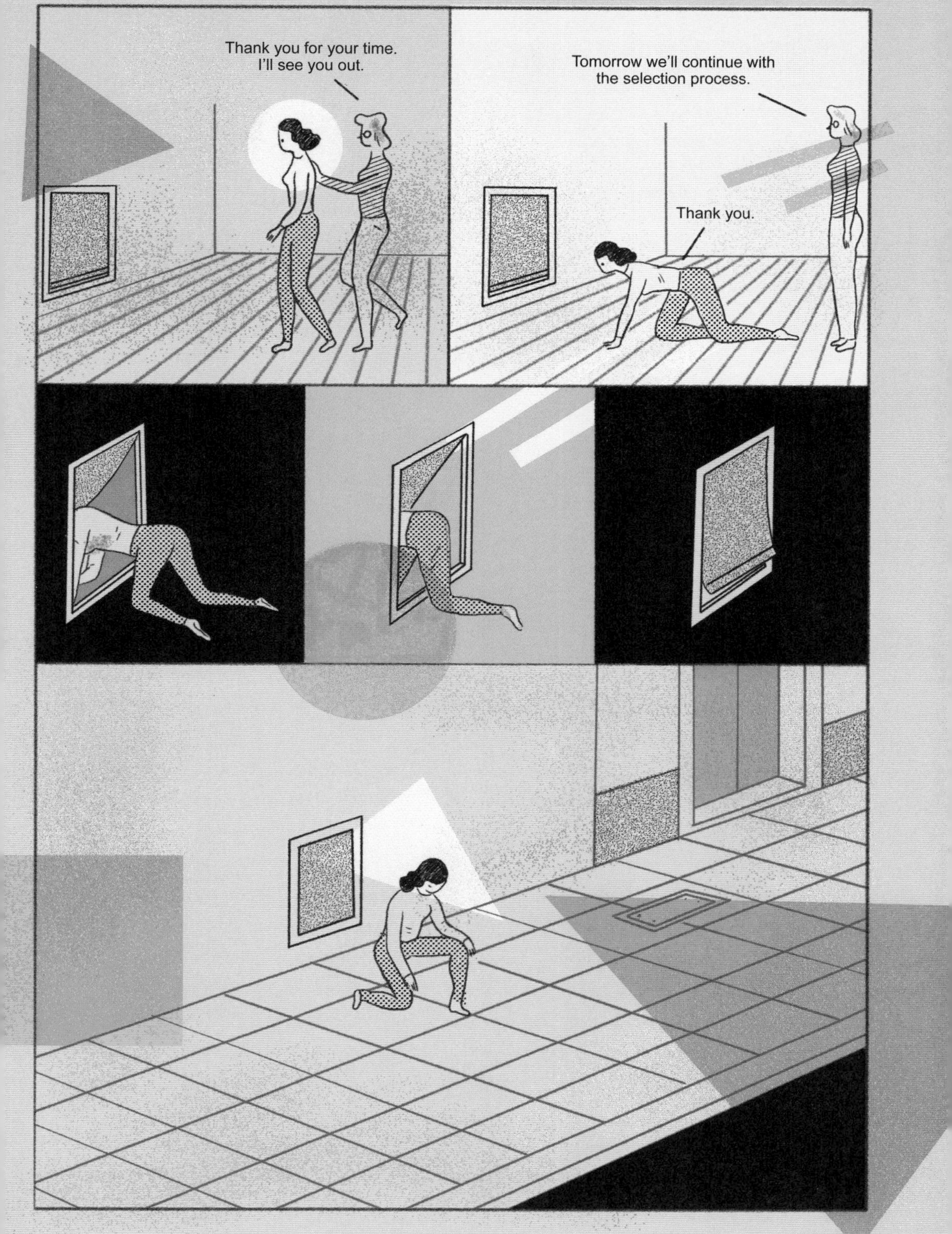
Thank you for your time.
I'll see you out.
Tomorrow we'll continue with
the selection process.
Thank you.

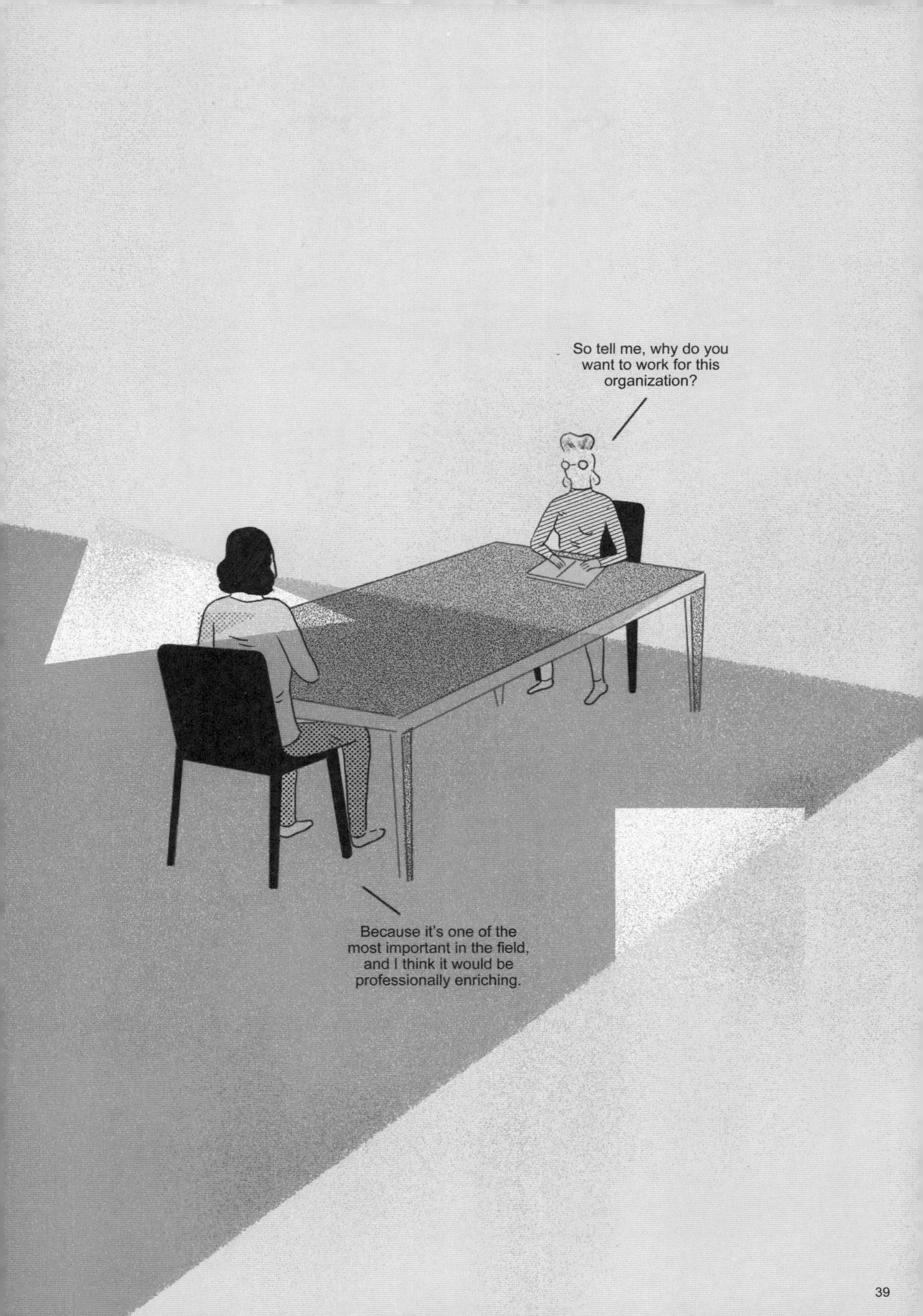
So tell me, why do you want to work for this organization?
Because it's one of the most important in the field, and I think it would be professionally enriching.

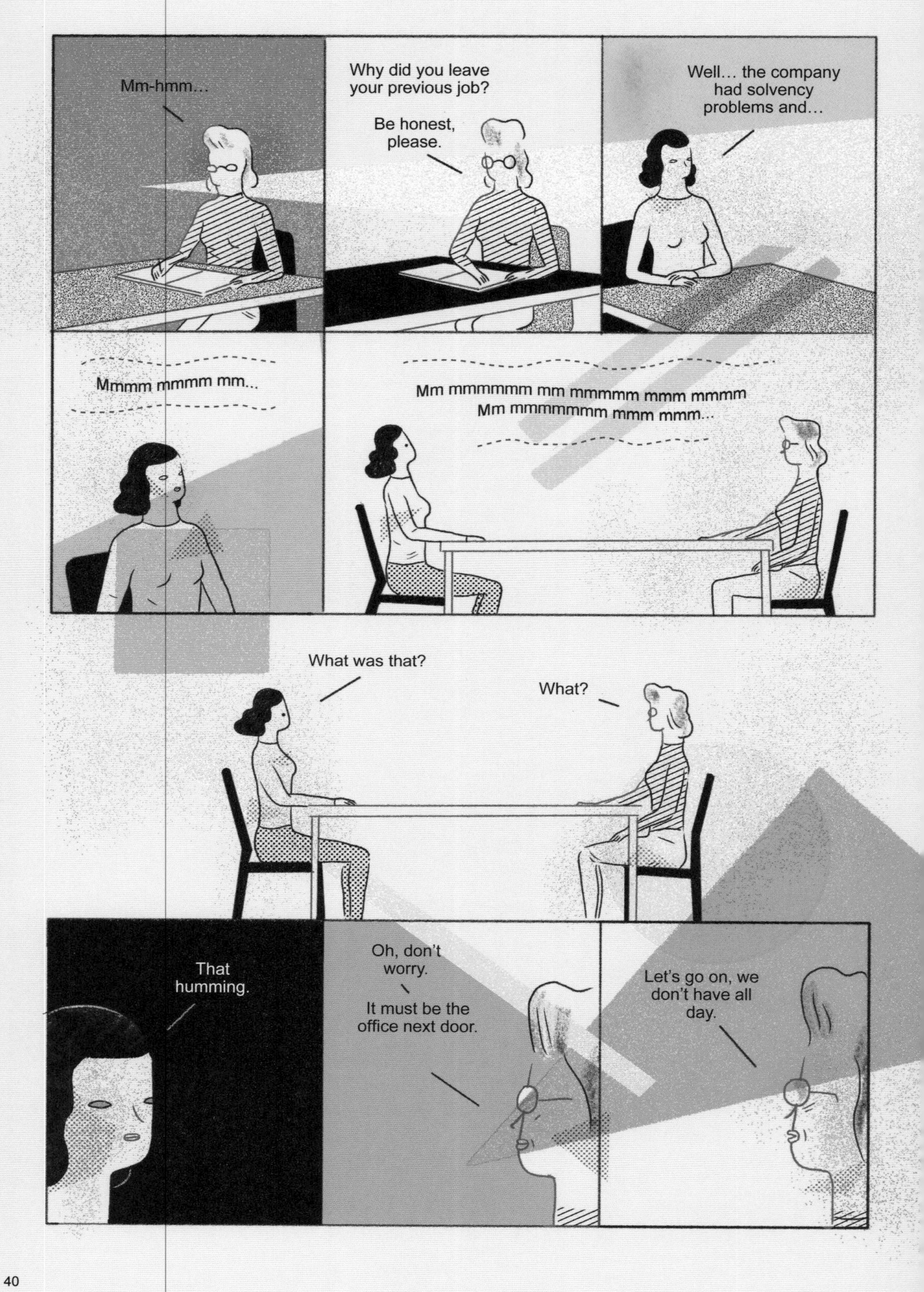
Mm-hmm…
Why did you leave your previous job?
Be honest, please.
Well… the company had solvency problems and…
Mmmm mmmm mm…
Mm mmmmmm mm mmmmm mmm mmmm
Mm mmmmmmm mmm mmm…
What was that?
What?
That humming.
Oh, don't worry.
It must be the office next door.
Let's go on, we don't have all day.

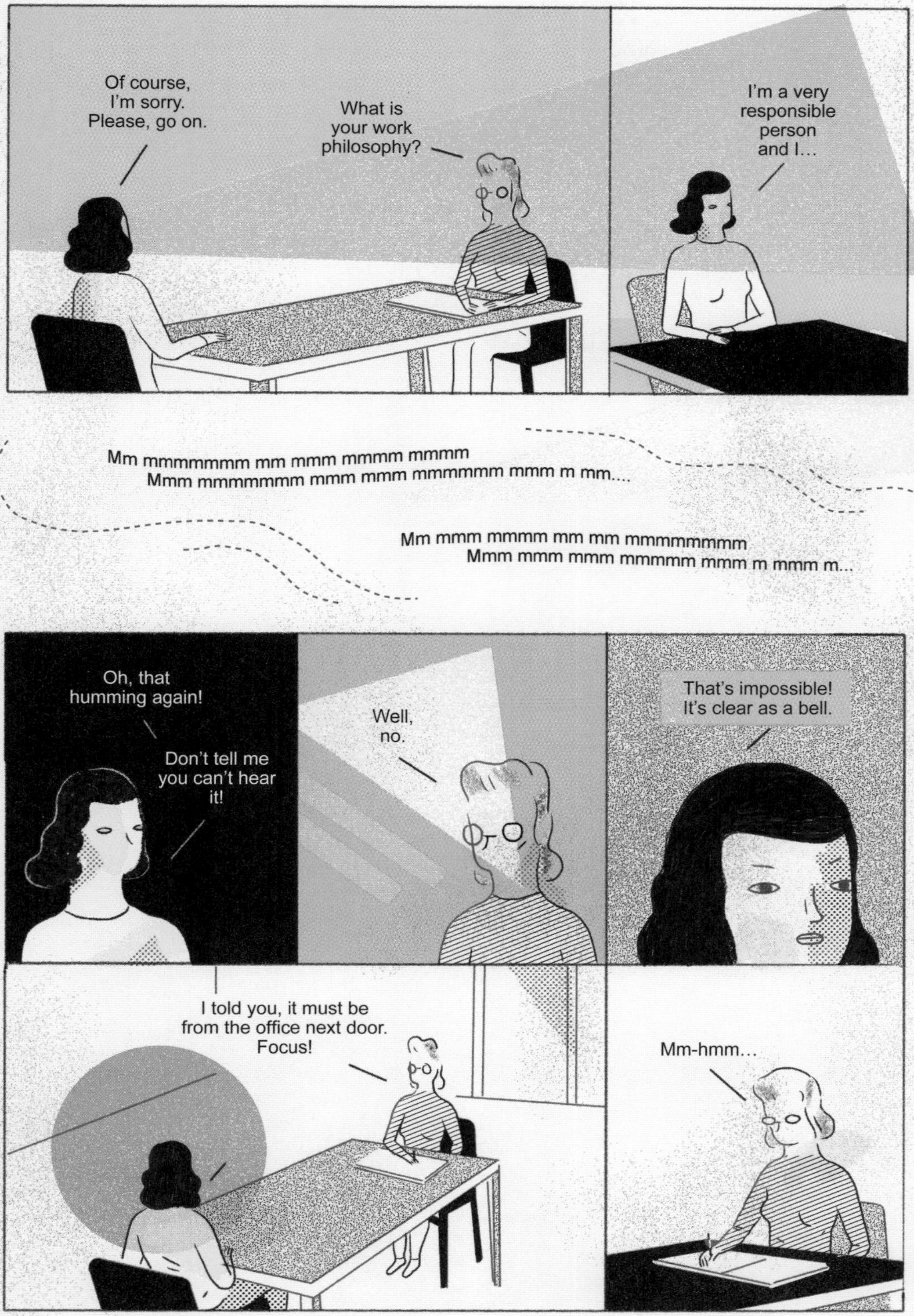

What is your work philosophy?
Of course, I'm sorry. Please, go on.
I'm a very responsible person and I...
Mm mmmmmmm mm mmm mmmm mmmm
Mmm mmmmmmm mmm mmm mmmmmm mmm m mm....
Mm mmm mmmm mm mm mmmmmmmm
Mmm mmm mmm mmmmm mmm m mmm m...
Oh, that humming again!
Don't tell me you can't hear it!
Well, no.
That's impossible! It's clear as a bell.
I told you, it must be from the office next door. Focus!
Mm-hmm...

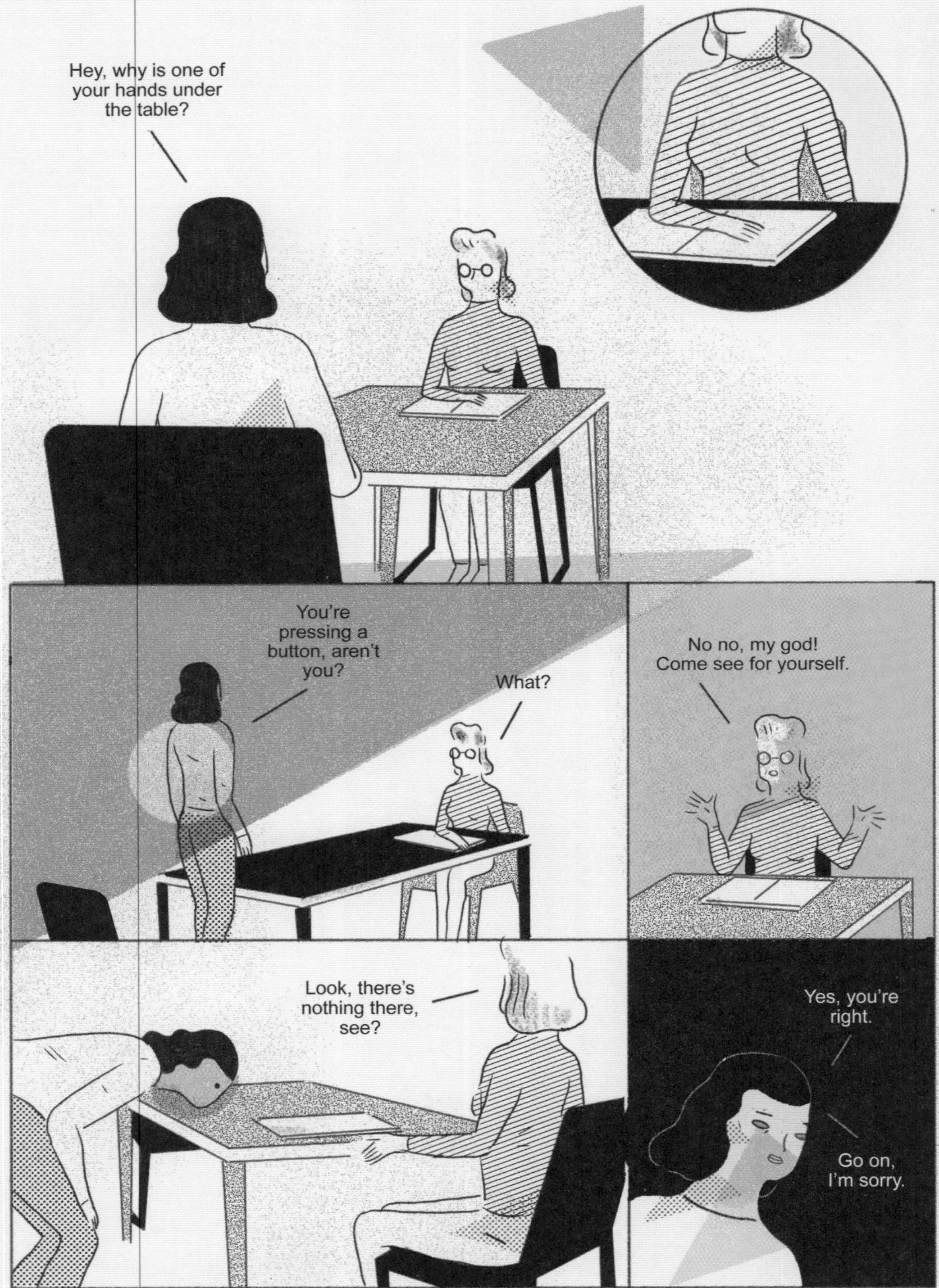
Hey, why is one of your hands under the table?
You're pressing a button, aren't you?
What?
No no, my god! Come see for yourself.
Look, there's nothing there, see?
Yes, you're right.
Go on, I'm sorry.

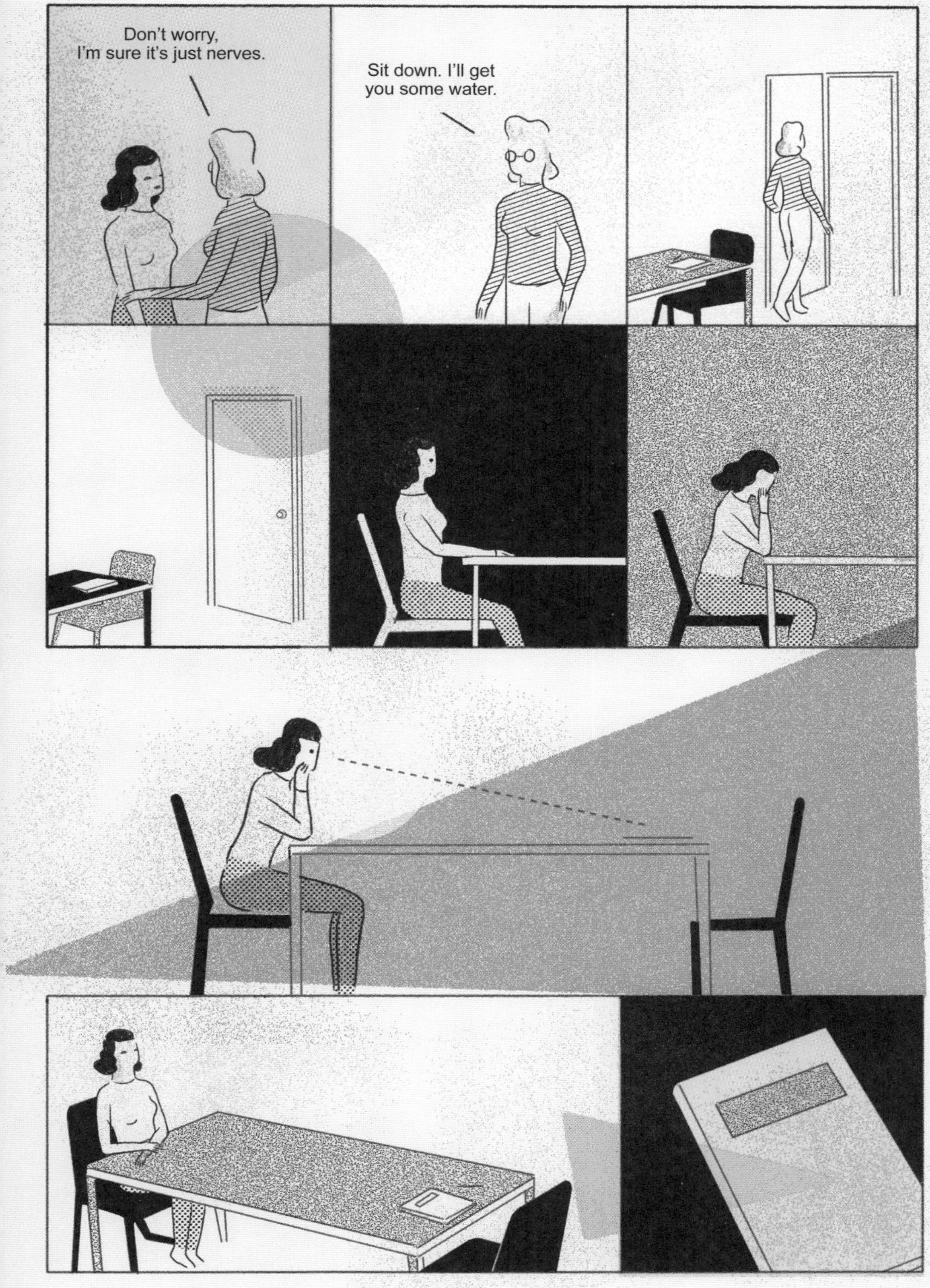
Don't worry,
I'm sure it's just nerves.
Sit down. I'll get
you some water.

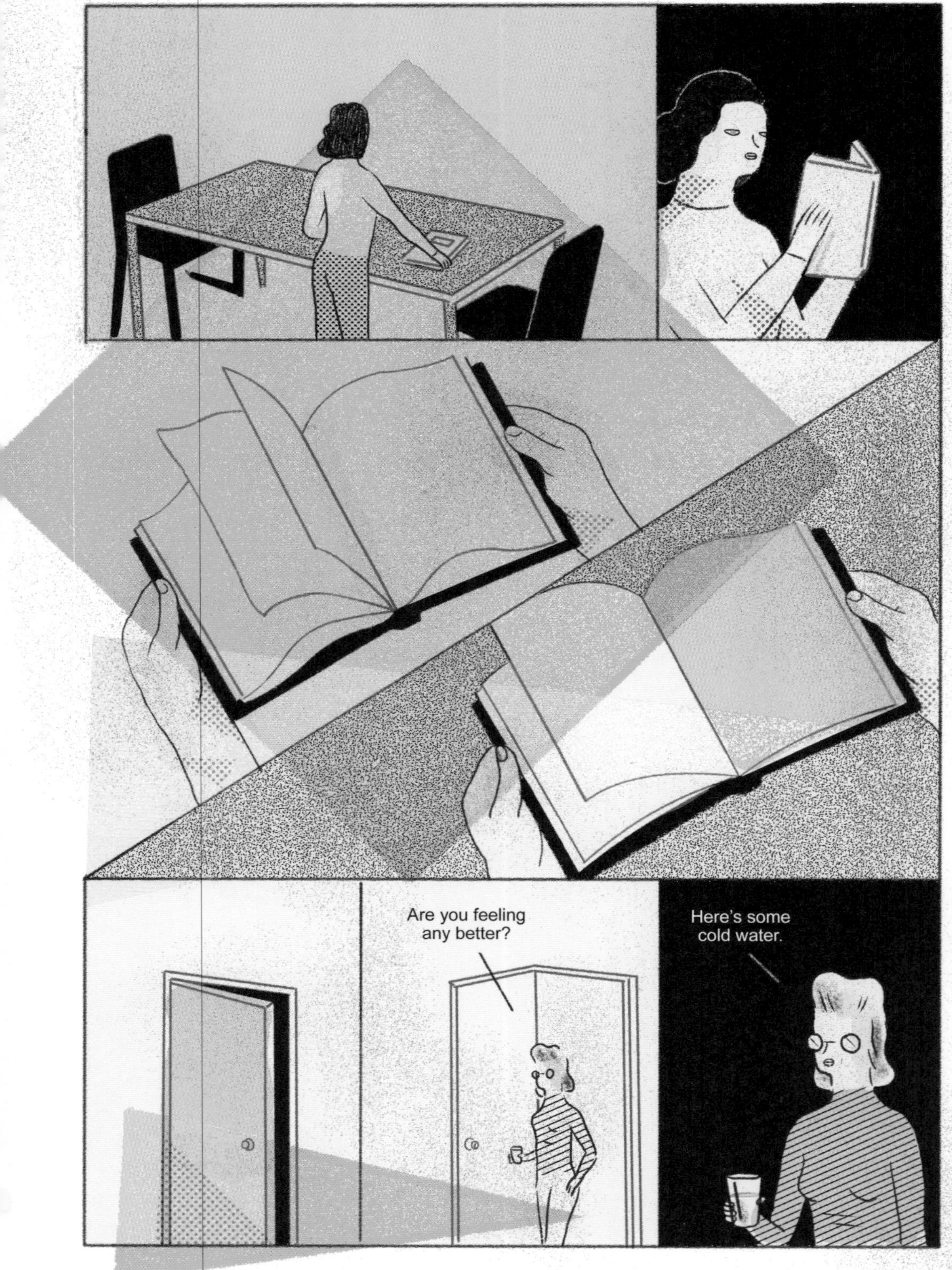
Are you feeling
any better?
Here's some
cold water.

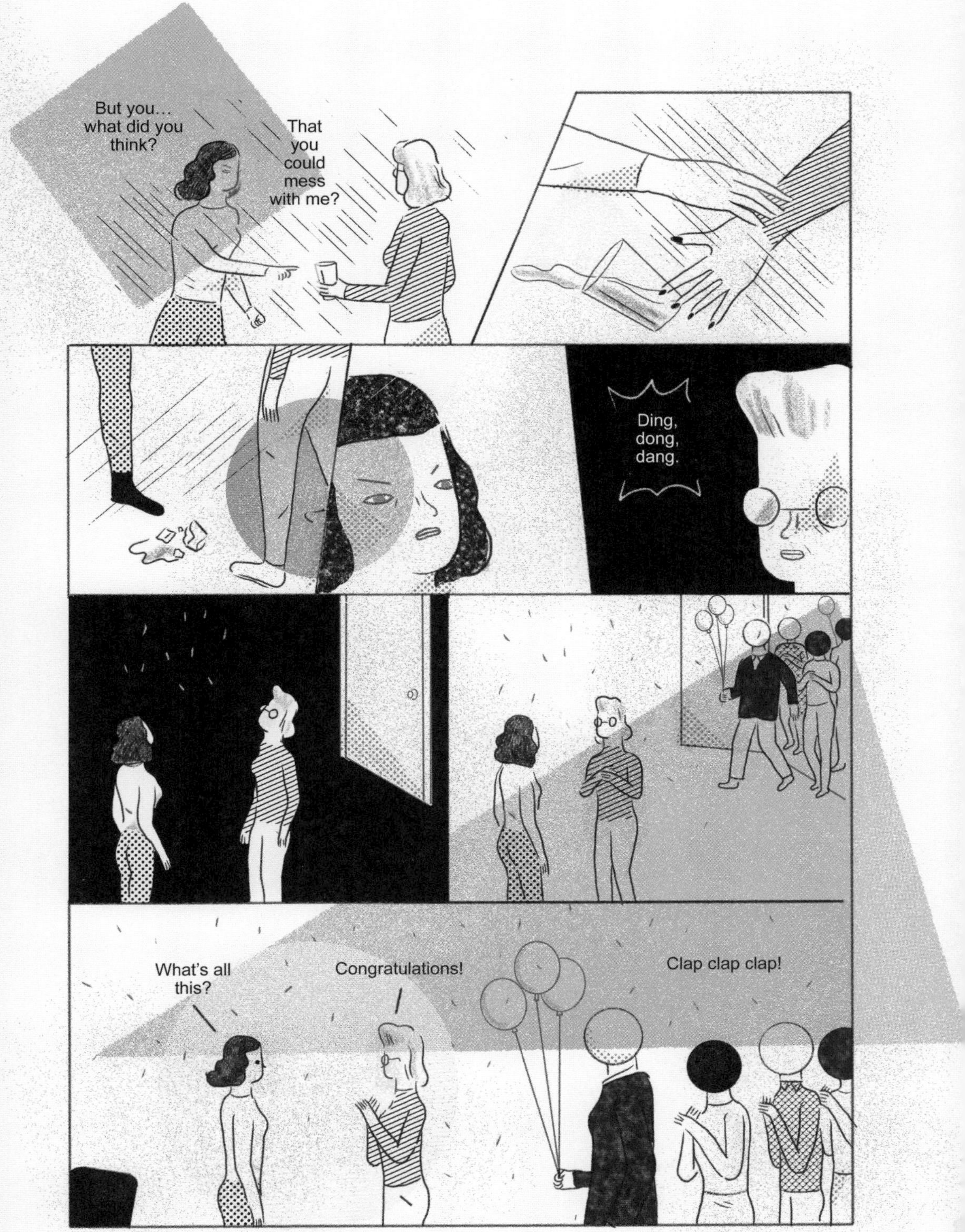

But you… what did you think?
That you could mess with me?
Ding, dong, dang.
What's all this?
Congratulations!
Clap clap clap!

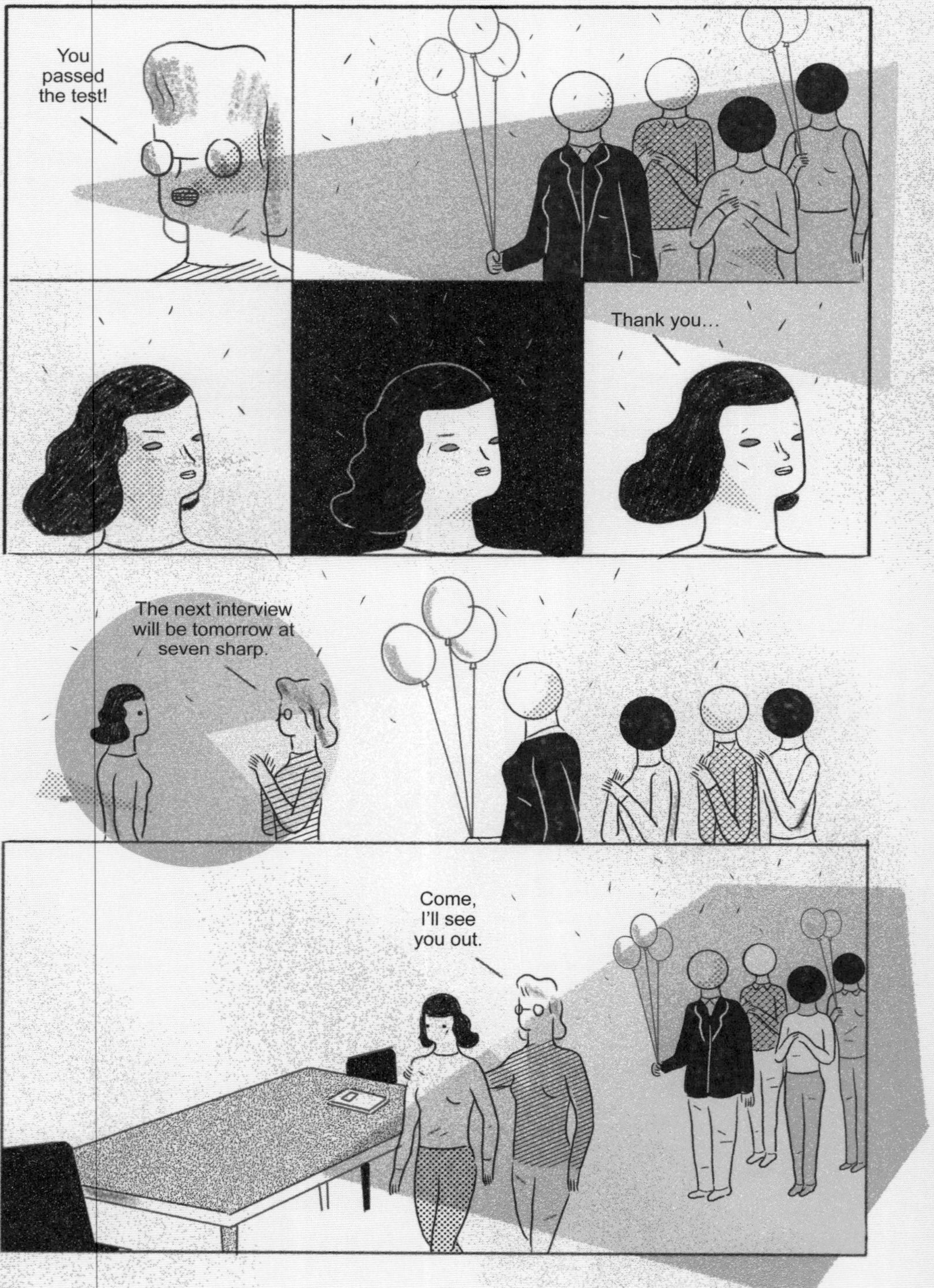
You passed the test!
Thank you...
The next interview will be tomorrow at seven sharp.
Come, I'll see you out.

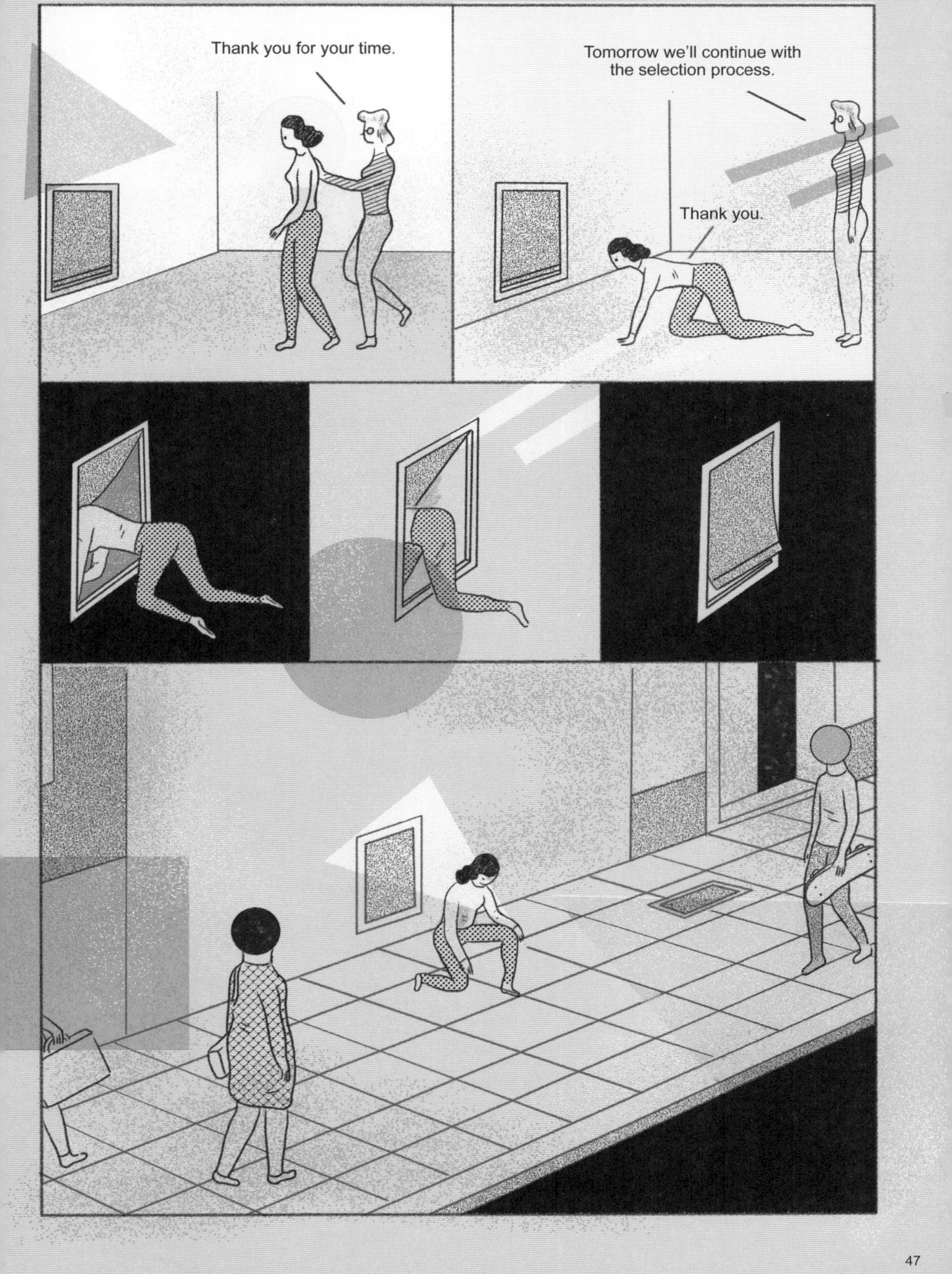
Thank you for your time.
Tomorrow we'll continue with the selection process.
Thank you.

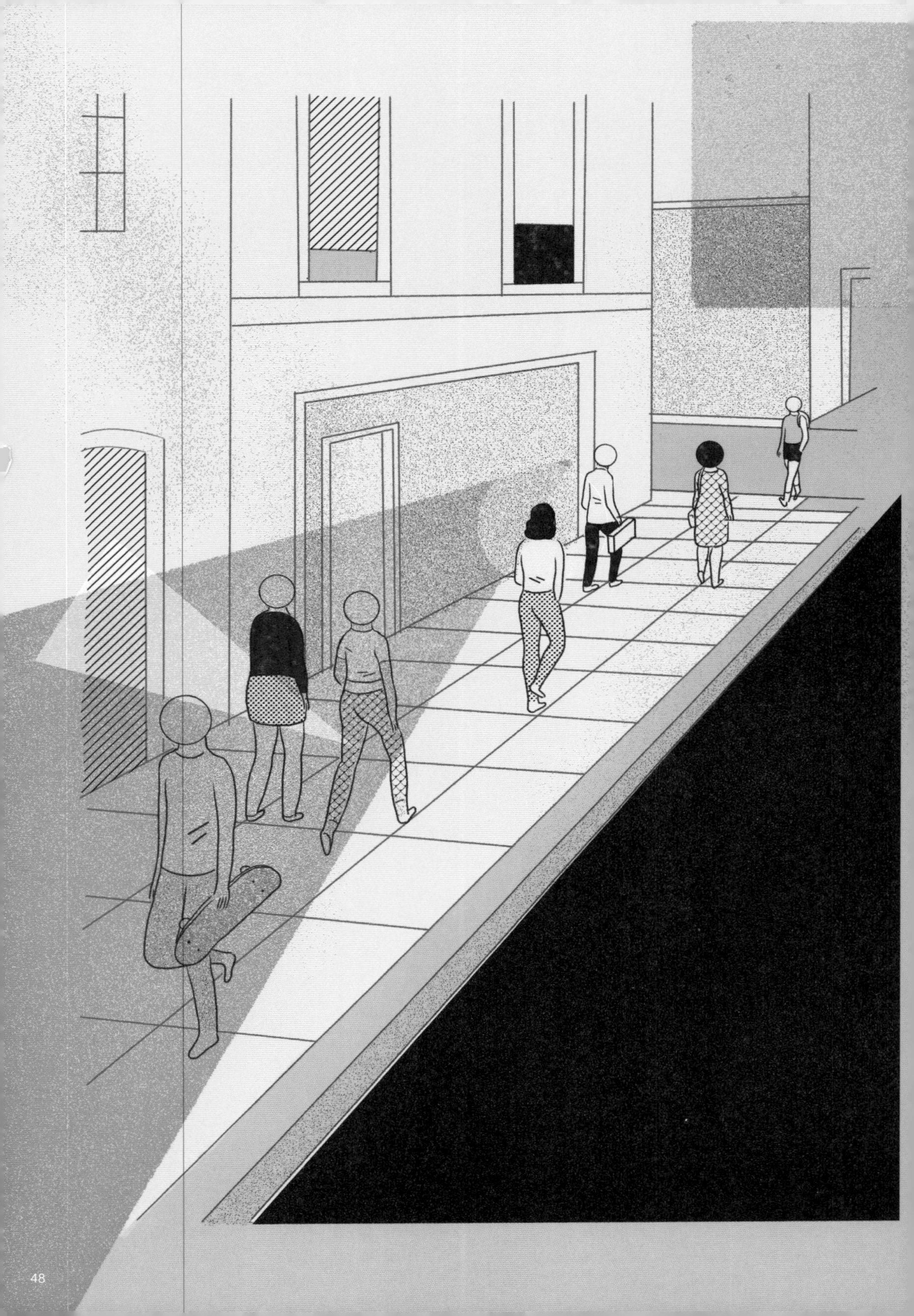

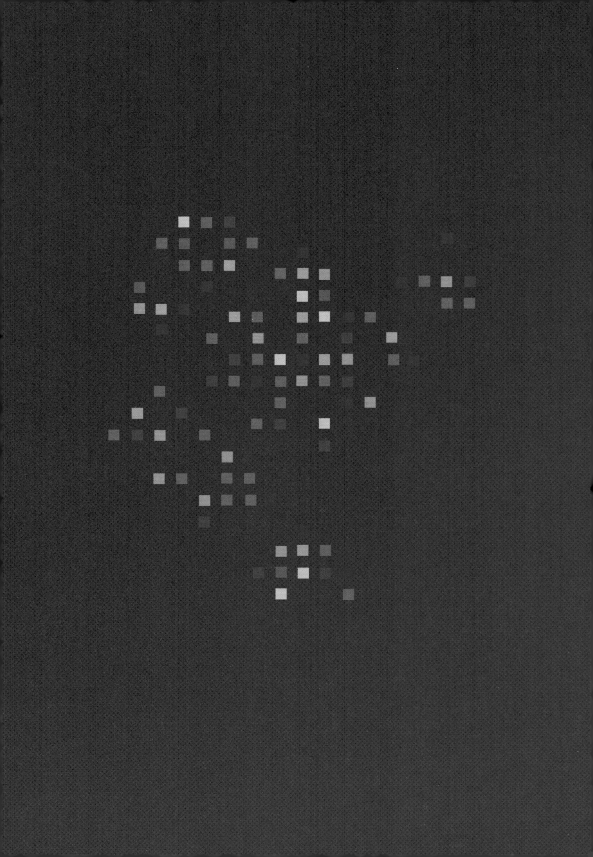

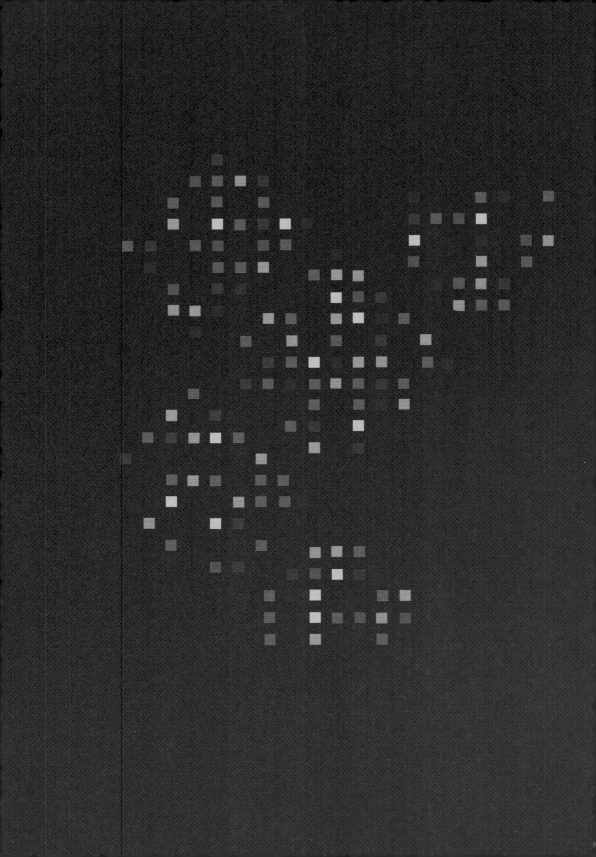

Here, Father 734δ is much older and sadder.
I really miss him…

The day I arrived, your pet kept barking at me. She was the only one who noticed.

I'll take good care of her.

Don't worry.

I can't imagine what it's like for you… I hope you've gotten used to it, too.

It's strange, the landscapes are so similar here, but so different in the details…

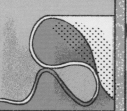

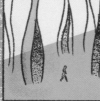

I think a lot about last spring…

Yet there are days when I doubt that all of it was real.

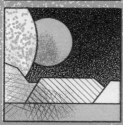

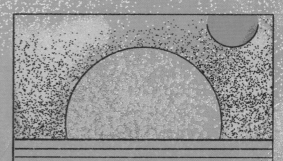

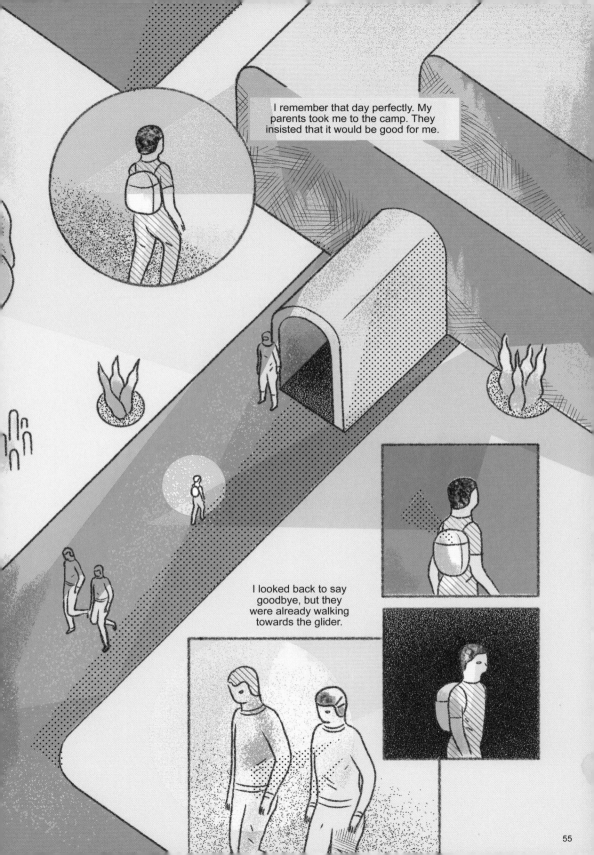

I remember that day perfectly. My parents took me to the camp. They insisted that it would be good for me.

I looked back to say goodbye, but they were already walking towards the glider.

They put me in a uniform and I passed through a liquid crystal door.
Once I had crossed over, there was no way to turn back.

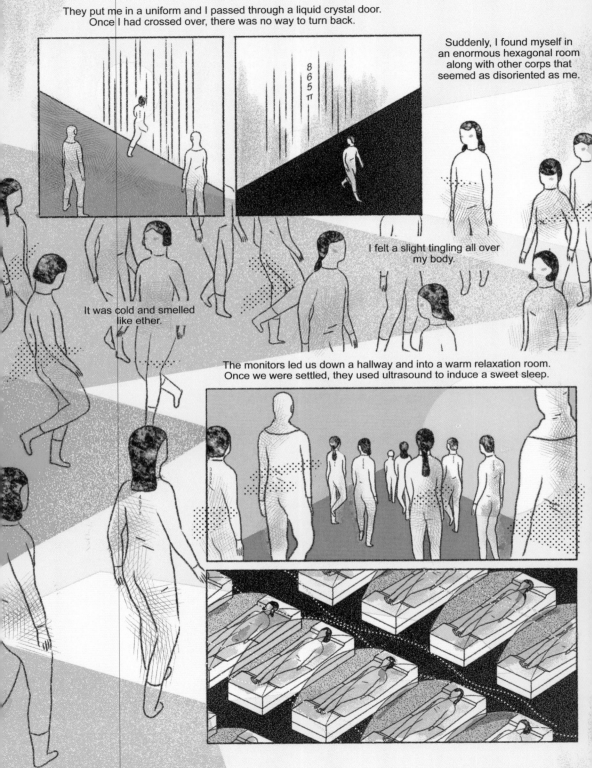

Suddenly, I found myself in an enormous hexagonal room along with other corps that seemed as disoriented as me.

I felt a slight tingling all over my body.

It was cold and smelled like ether.

The monitors led us down a hallway and into a warm relaxation room.
Once we were settled, they used ultrasound to induce a sweet sleep.

The next day, they ran exhaustive tests on us.

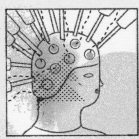  

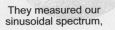
They measured our
sinusoidal spectrum,

somatosensory
balance,

and our bilocationary
abilities, among other things.

Between one test and the next, we furtively observed each other.

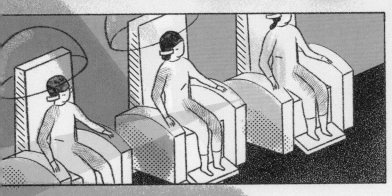

And at the end of the day, we had realized.

The activities went on, becoming idle.

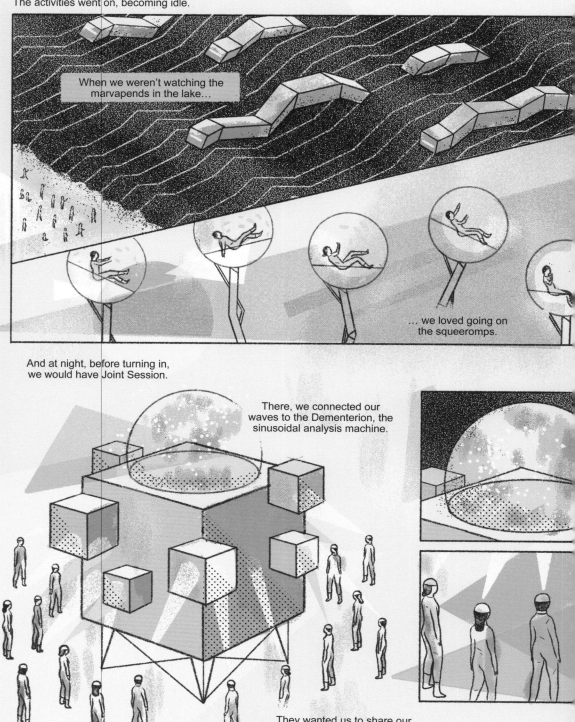

When we weren't watching the marvapends in the lake…

… we loved going on the squeeromps.

And at night, before turning in, we would have Joint Session.

There, we connected our waves to the Dementerion, the sinusoidal analysis machine.

They wanted us to share our experiences and abilities.

The machine analyzed all our data during camp.

And so, day by day, spring passed as if were a dream.

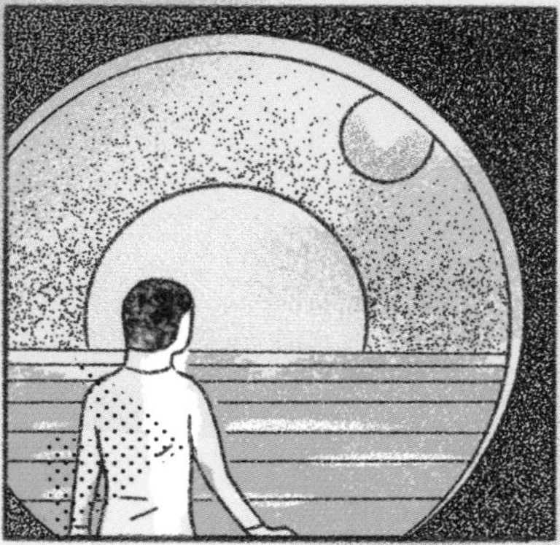

The monitors kept their distance. They only interacted with us for technical matters.

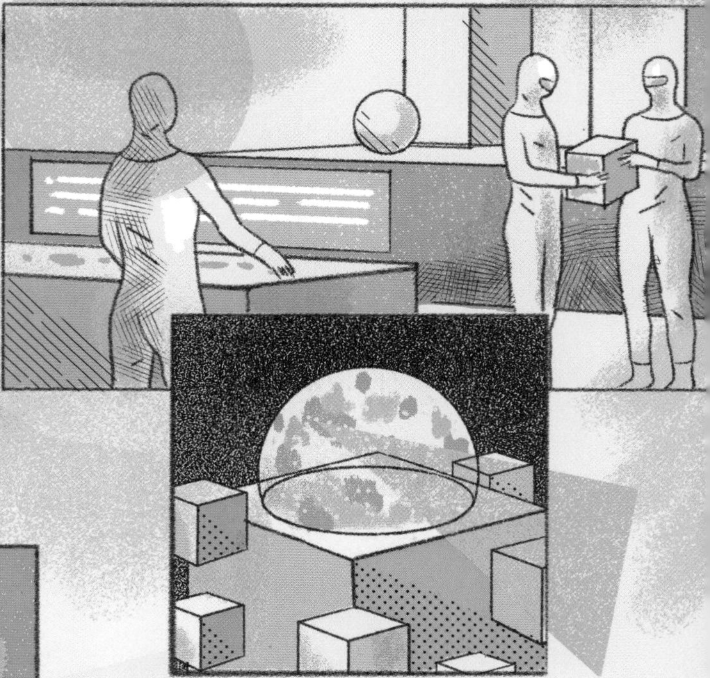

Meanwhile, The Shredder (as we called it) analyzed all our data.

Our thoughts, memories, and feelings. Nothing escaped its scrutiny.

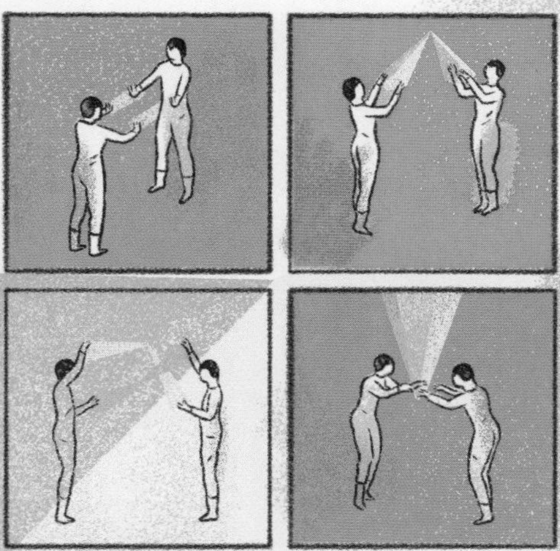

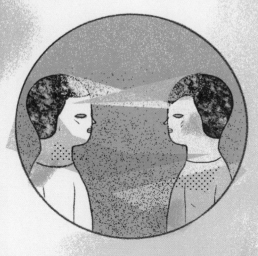

I spent all the time I could with you, 630Σ, attracted by what you had seen and experienced. All of it so foreign to my reality.

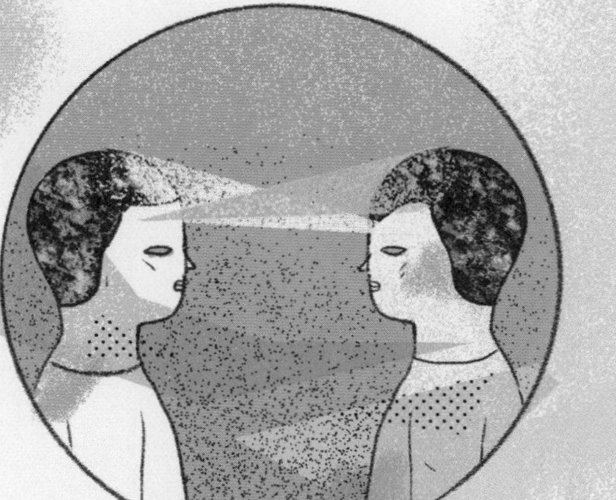

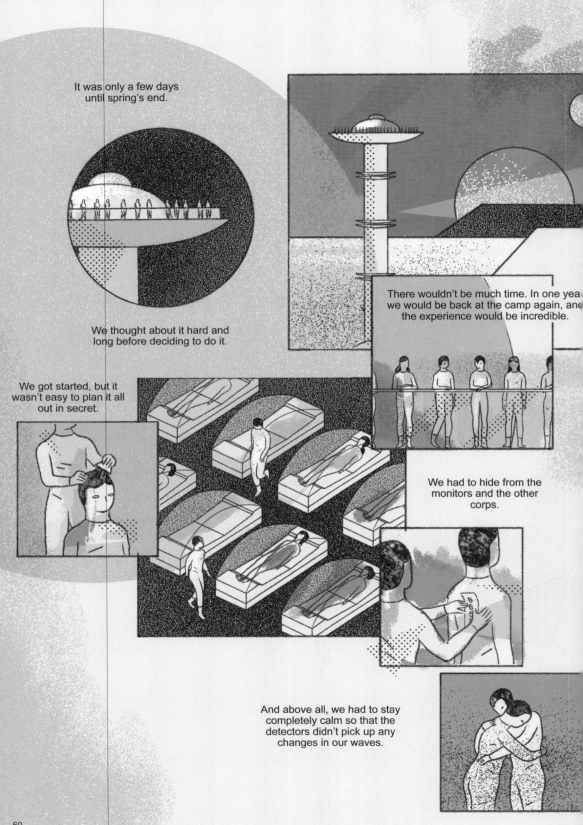

It was only a few days until spring's end.

We thought about it hard and long before deciding to do it.

There wouldn't be much time. In one year, we would be back at the camp again, and the experience would be incredible.

We got started, but it wasn't easy to plan it all out in secret.

We had to hide from the monitors and the other corps.

And above all, we had to stay completely calm so that the detectors didn't pick up any changes in our waves.

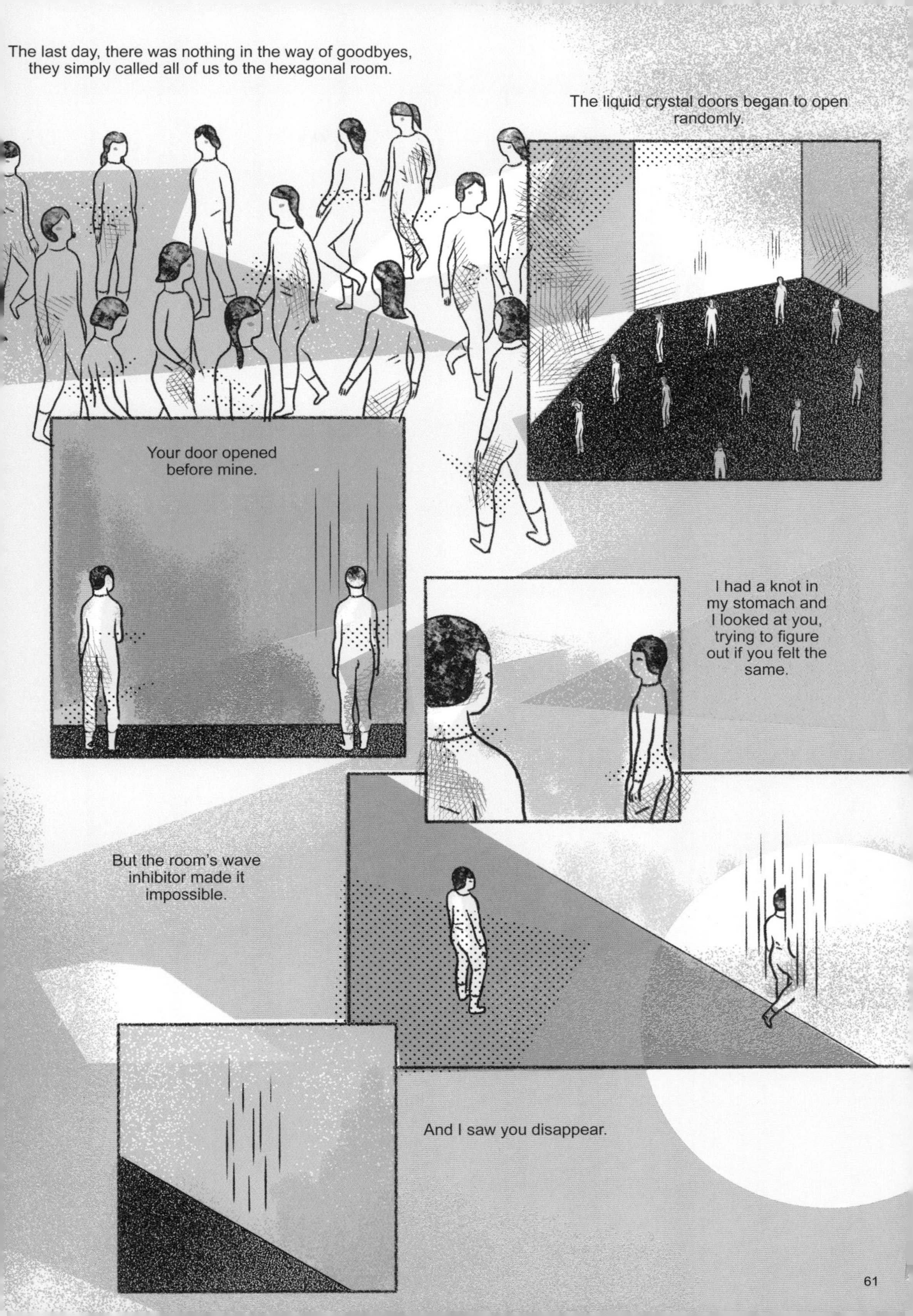
The last day, there was nothing in the way of goodbyes, they simply called all of us to the hexagonal room.
The liquid crystal doors began to open randomly.
Your door opened before mine.
I had a knot in my stomach and I looked at you, trying to figure out if you felt the same.
But the room's wave inhibitor made it impossible.
And I saw you disappear.

Without knowing that it would be forever.

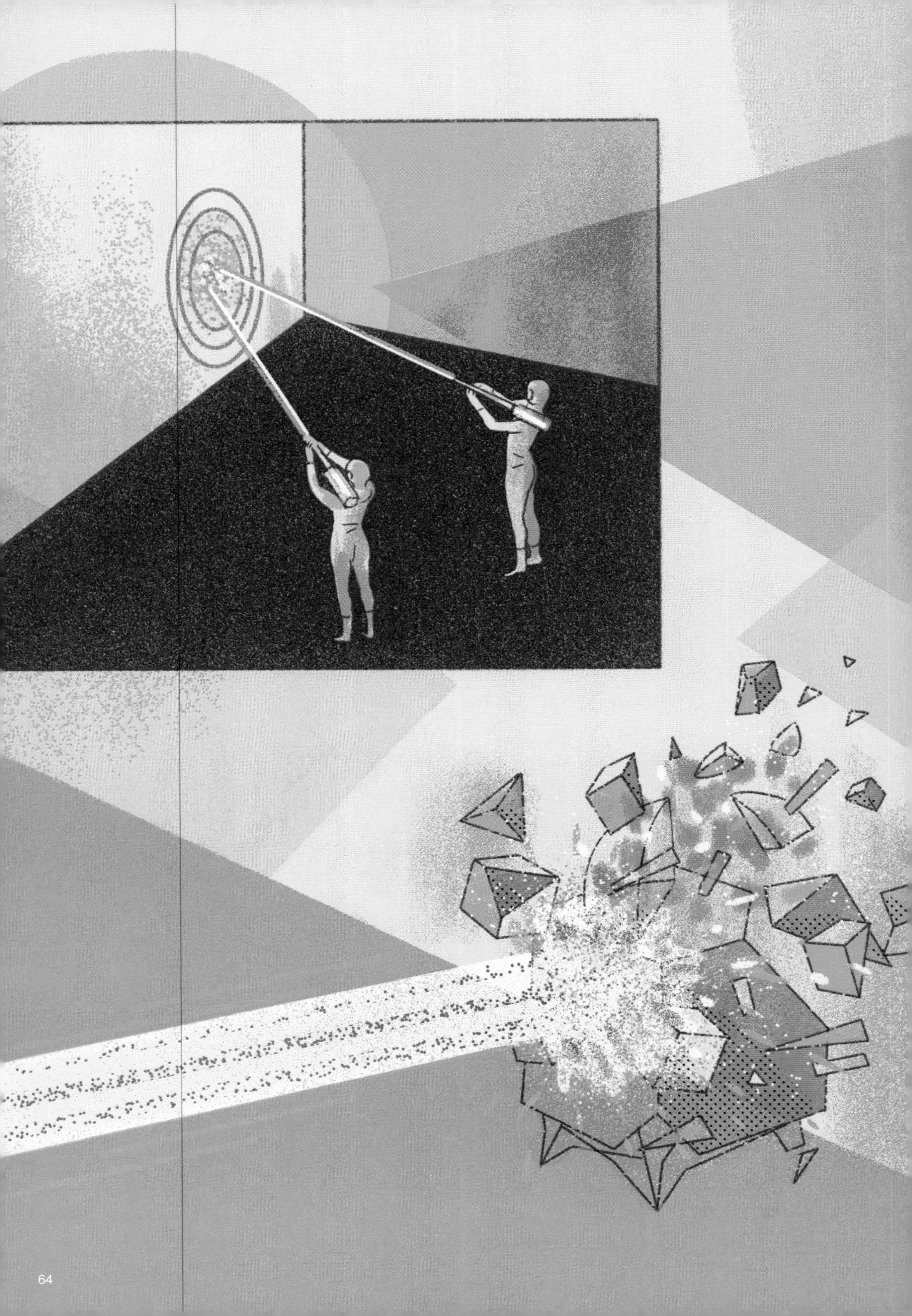

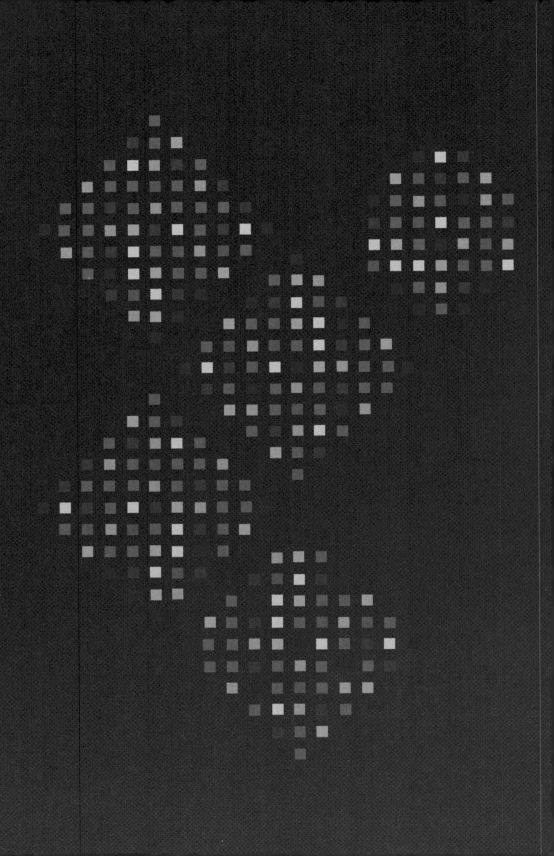

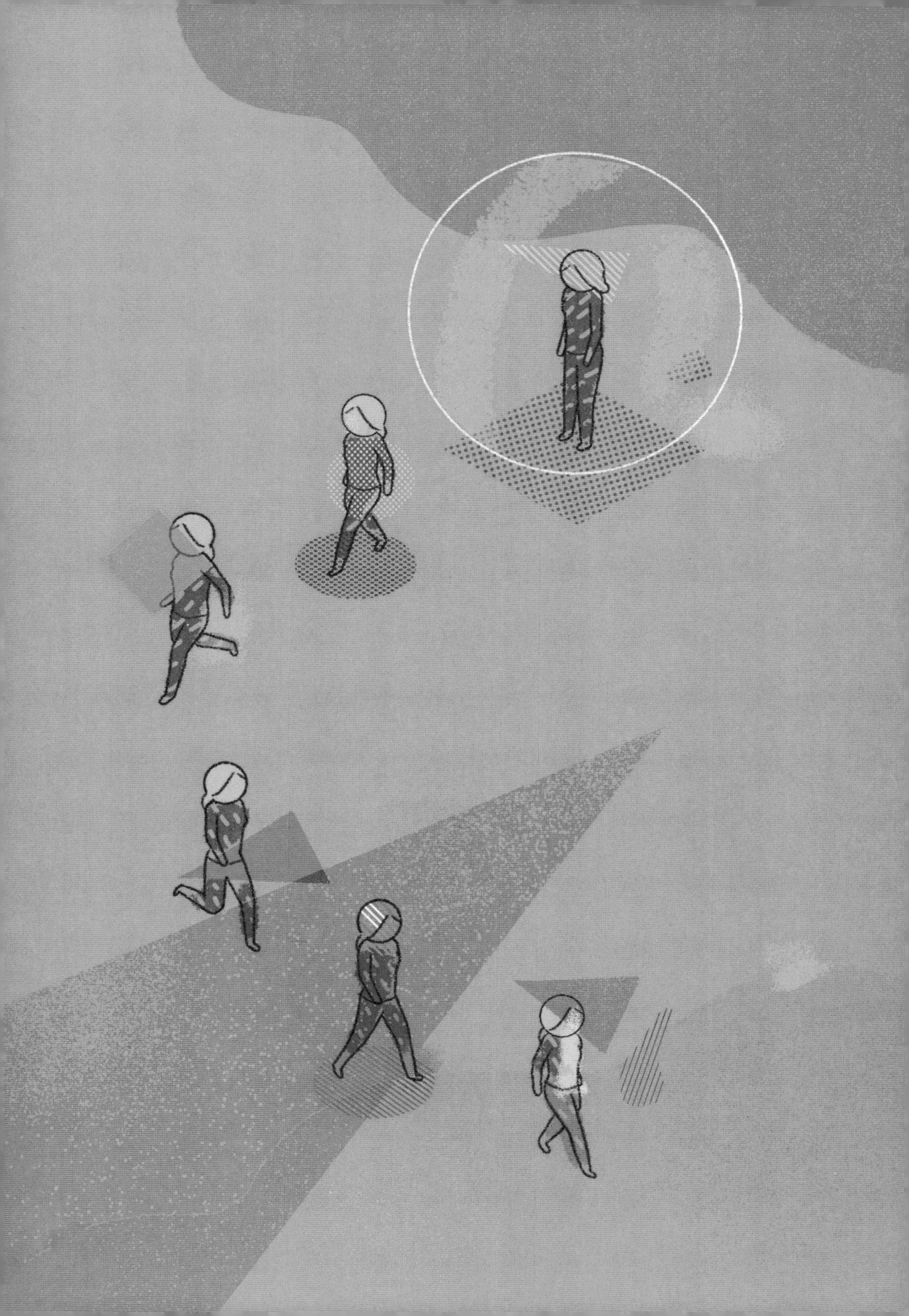

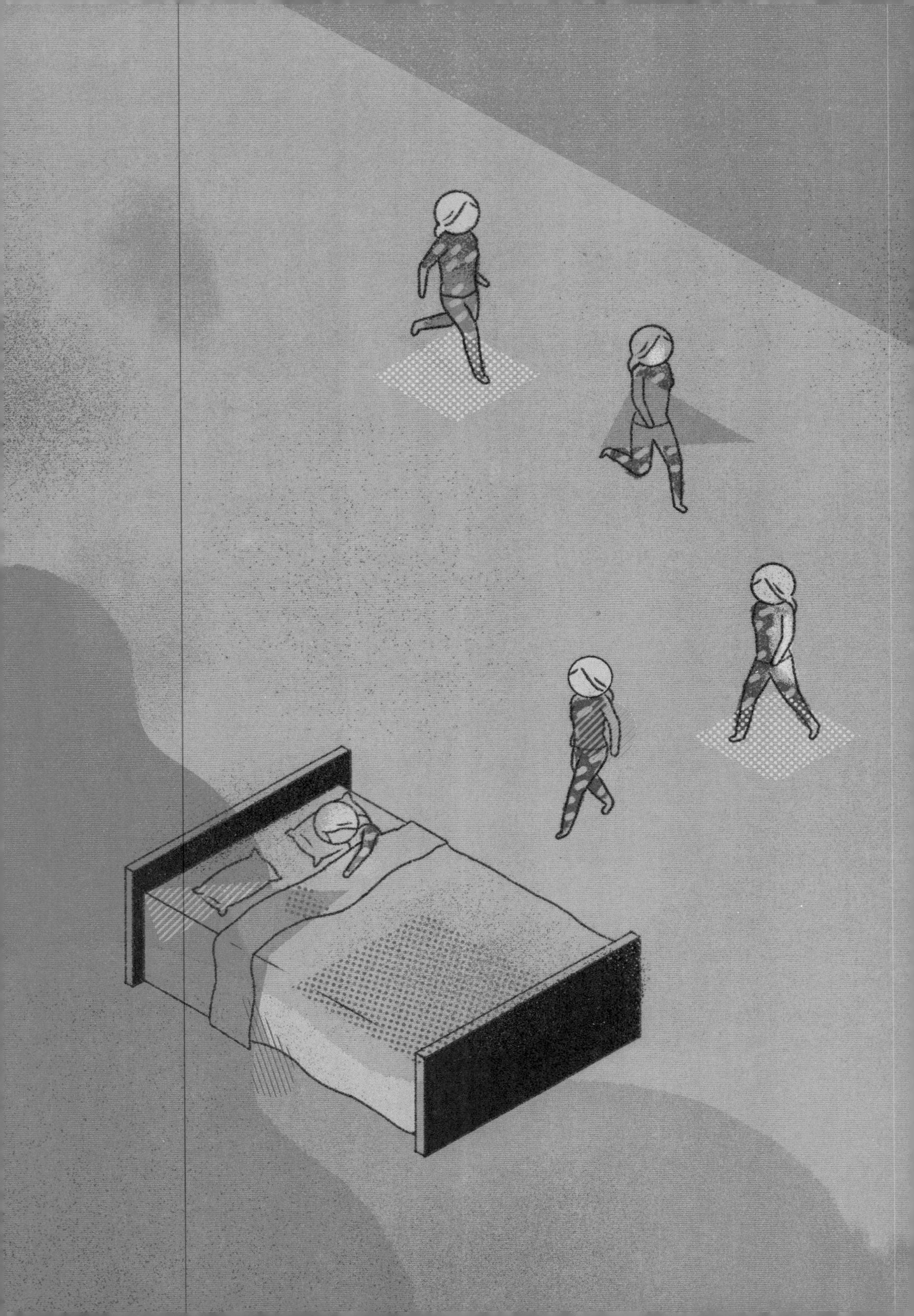

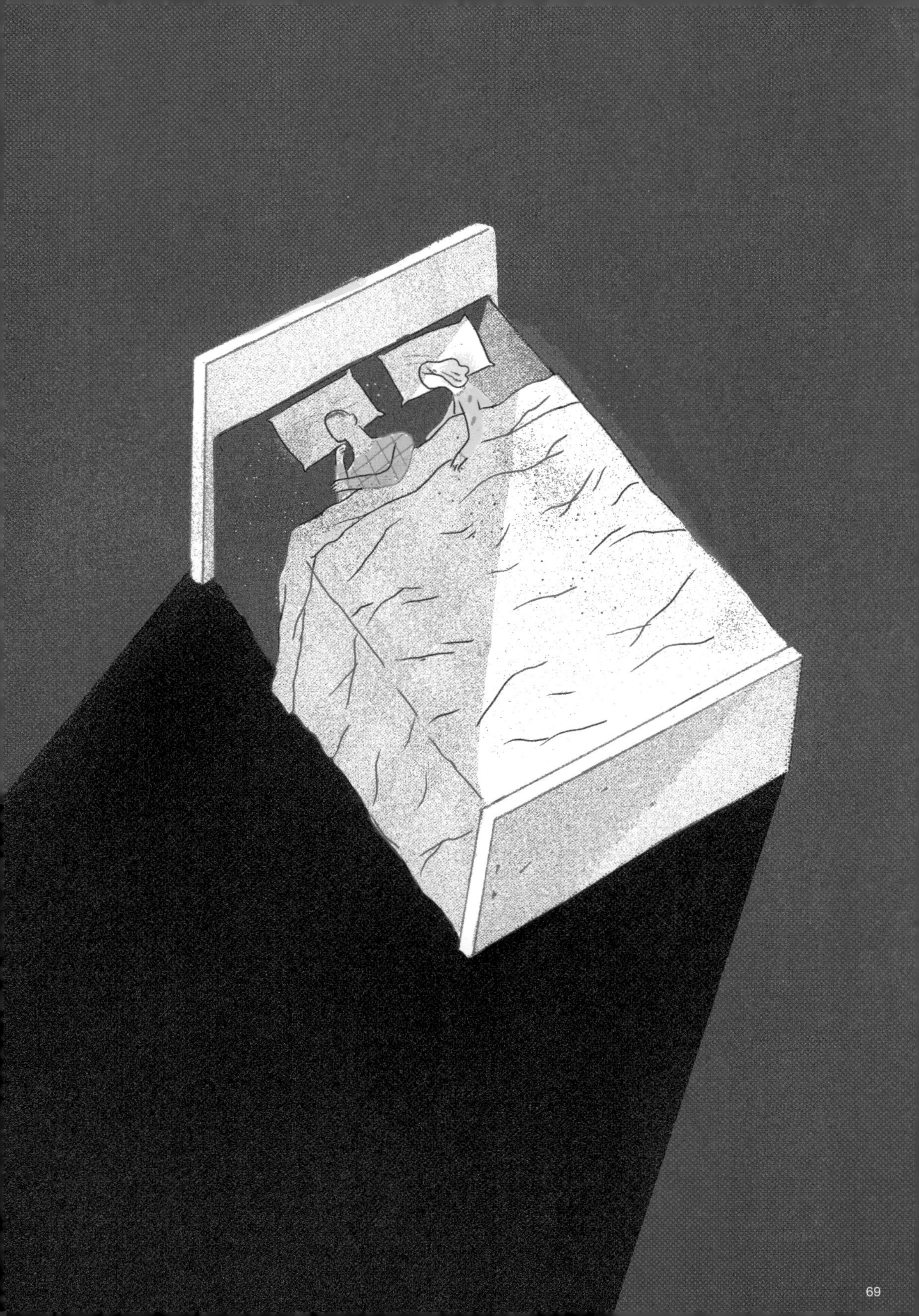

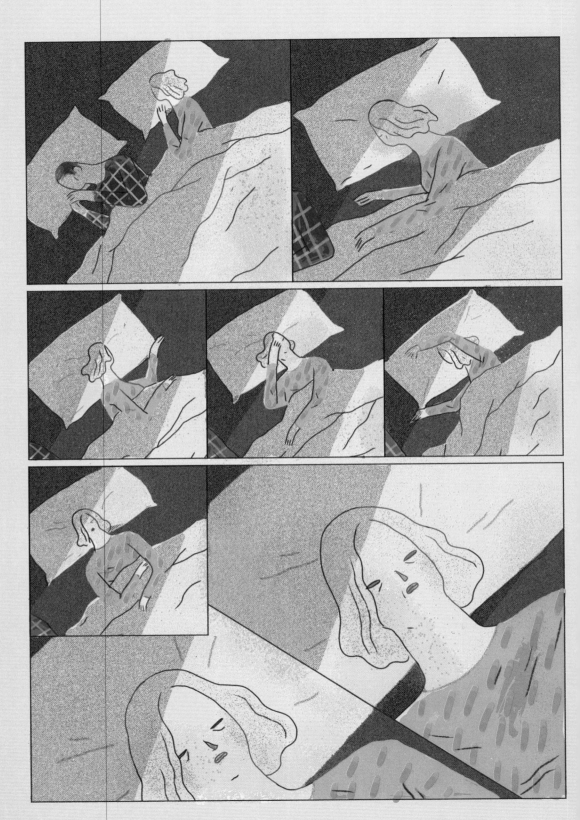

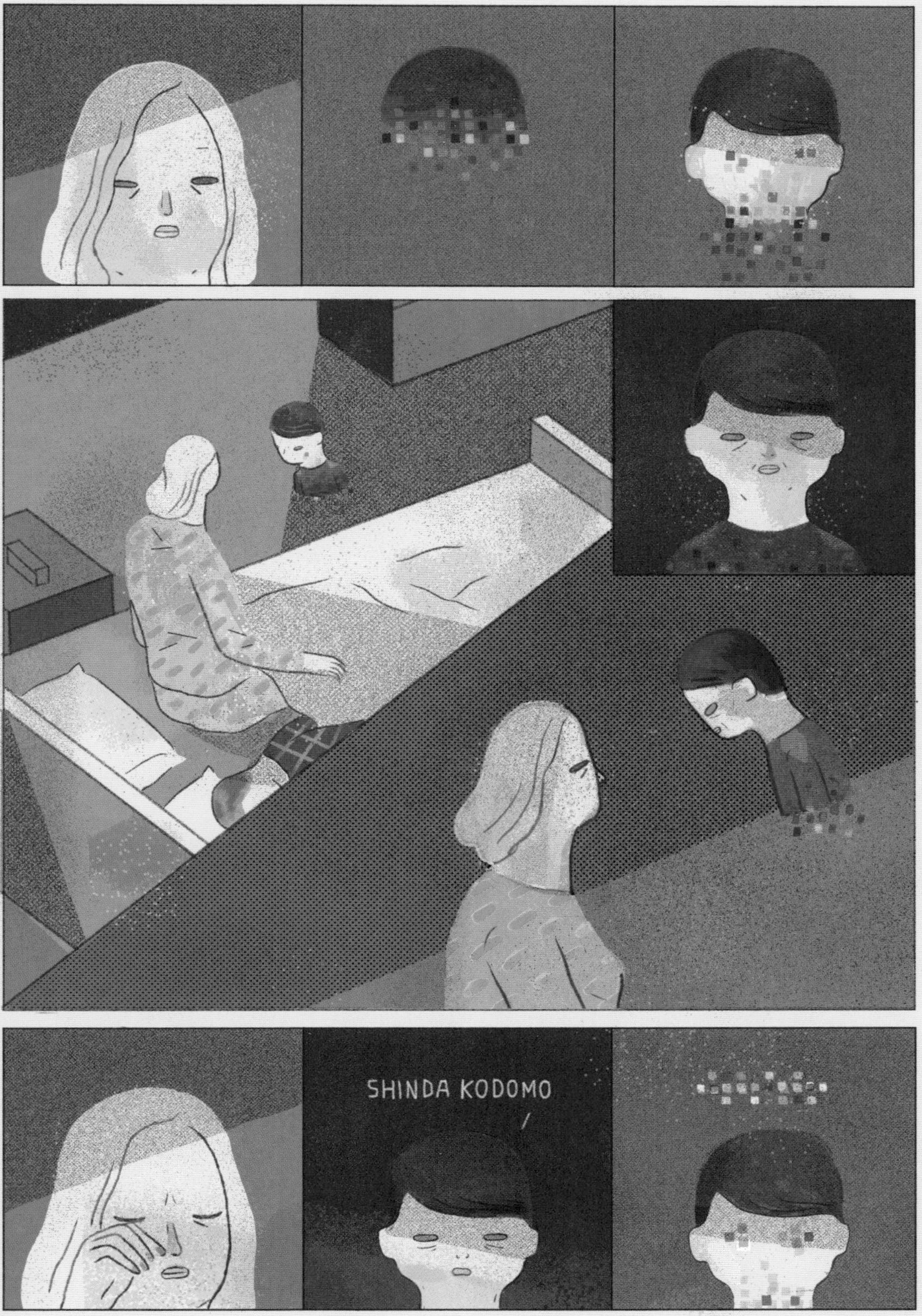
SHINDA KODOMO

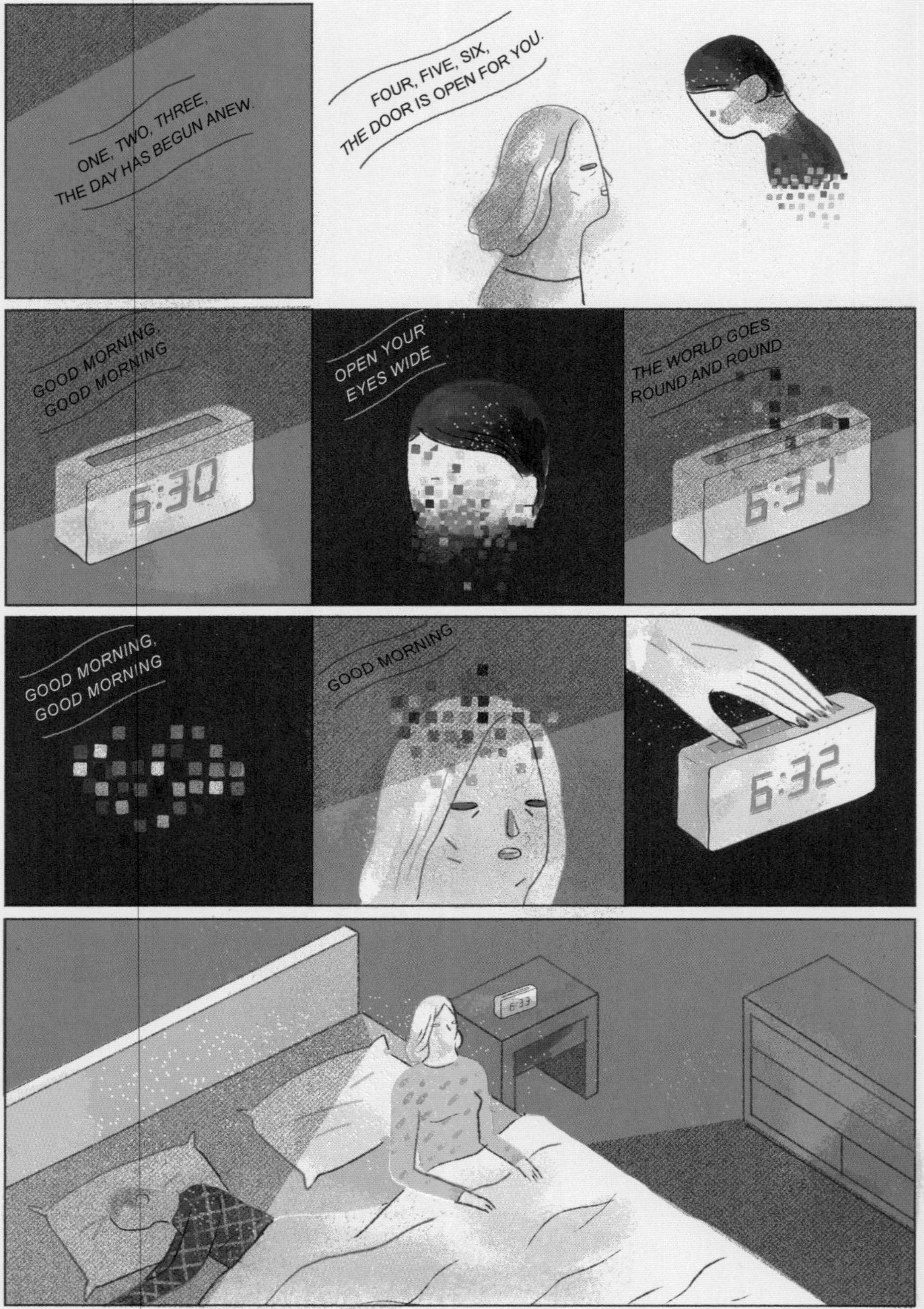
ONE, TWO, THREE,
THE DAY HAS BEGUN ANEW.
FOUR, FIVE, SIX,
THE DOOR IS OPEN FOR YOU.
GOOD MORNING,
GOOD MORNING
6:30
OPEN YOUR
EYES WIDE
THE WORLD GOES
ROUND AND ROUND
GOOD MORNING,
GOOD MORNING
GOOD MORNING
6:32
6:33

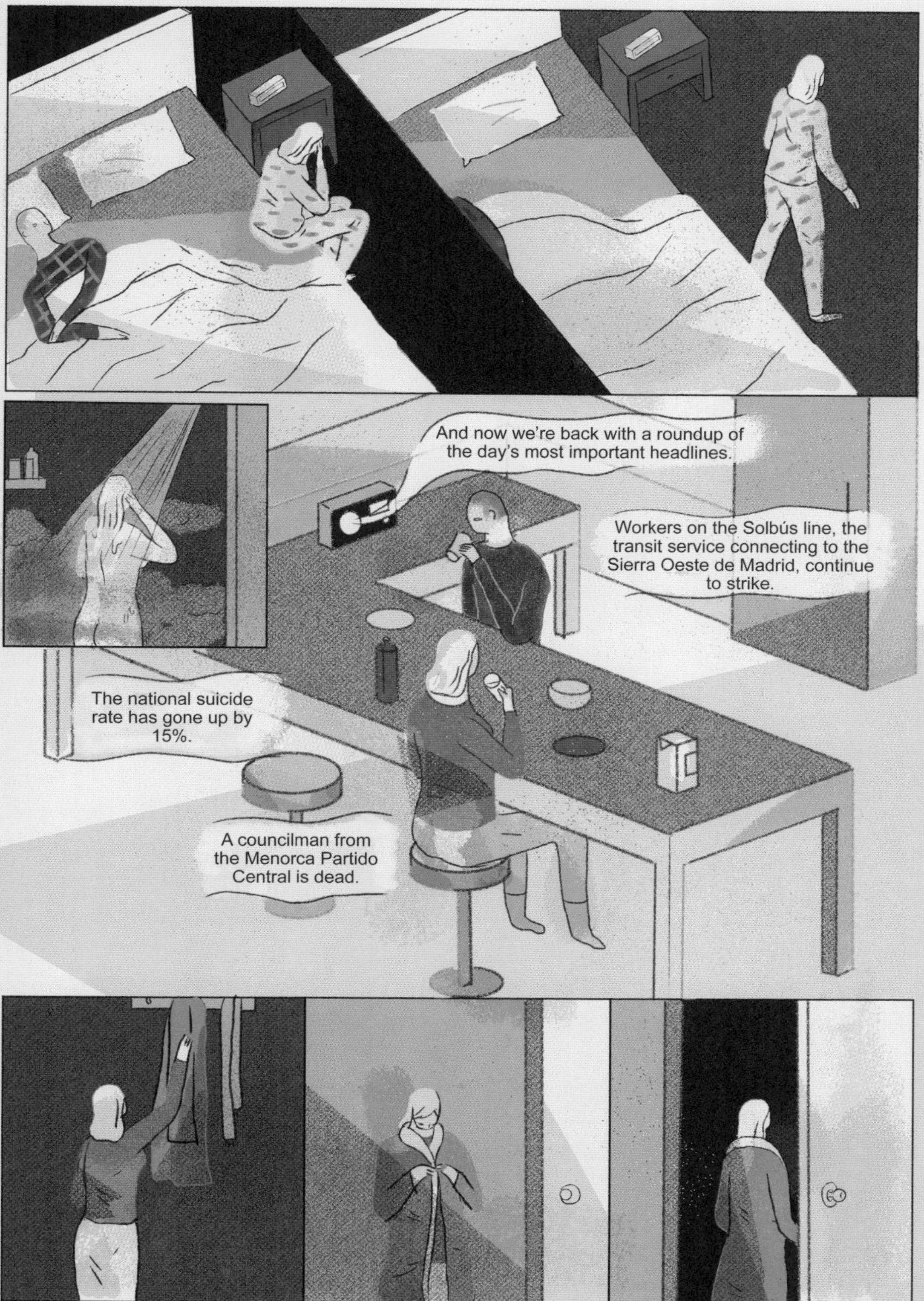

And now we're back with a roundup of the day's most important headlines.
Workers on the Solbús line, the transit service connecting to the Sierra Oeste de Madrid, continue to strike.
The national suicide rate has gone up by 15%.
A councilman from the Menorca Partido Central is dead.

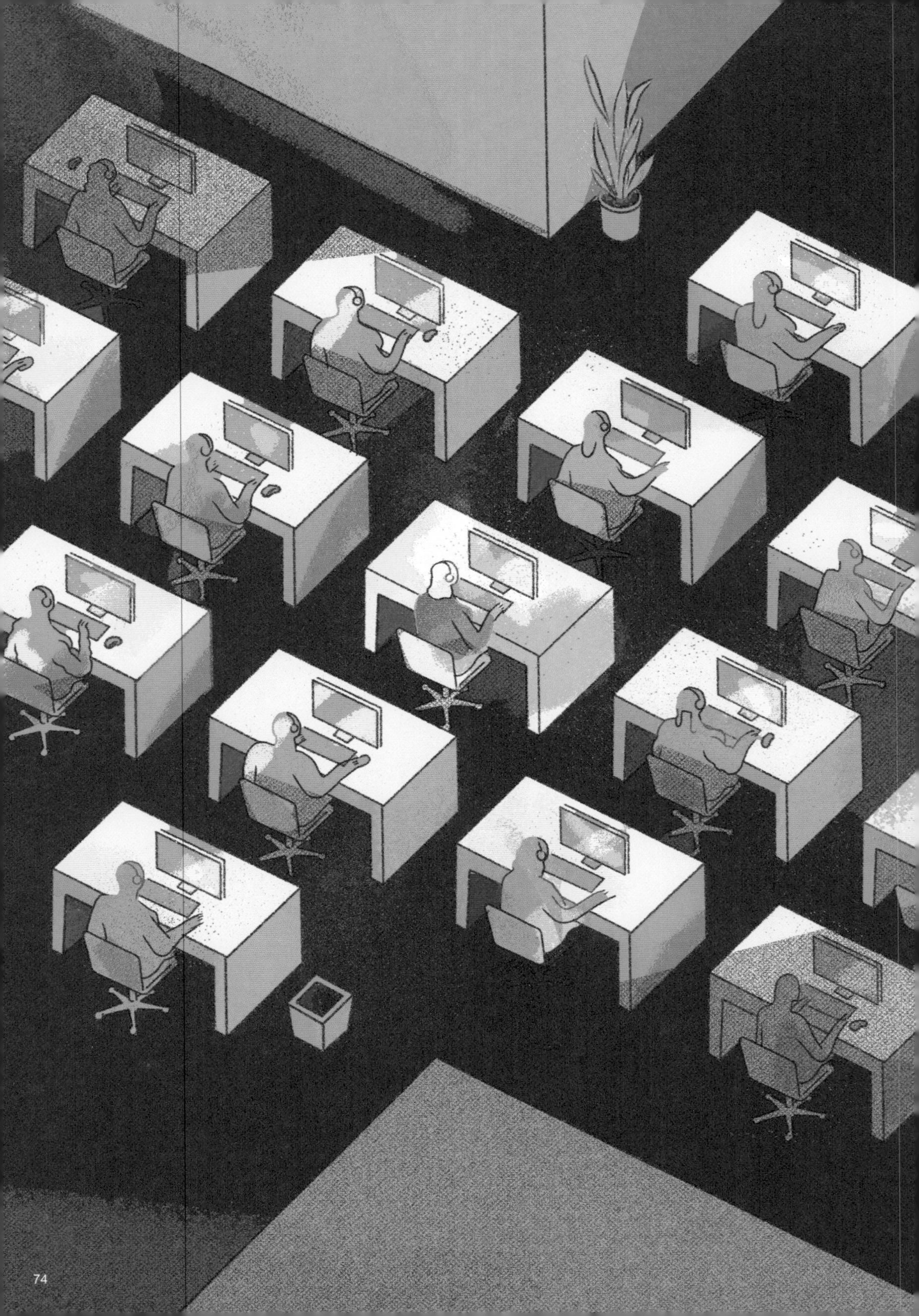

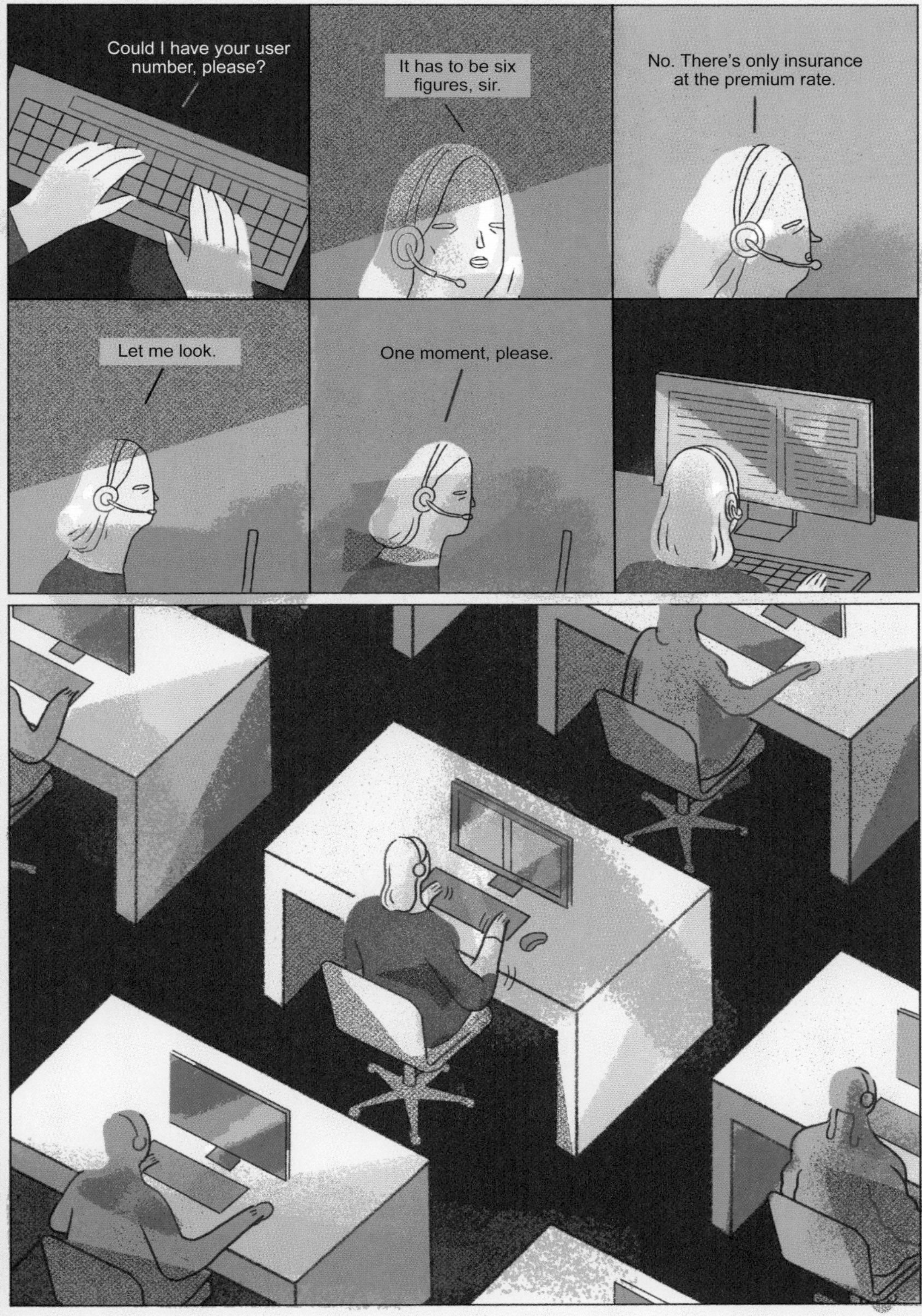
Could I have your user number, please?
It has to be six figures, sir.
No. There's only insurance at the premium rate.
Let me look.
One moment, please.

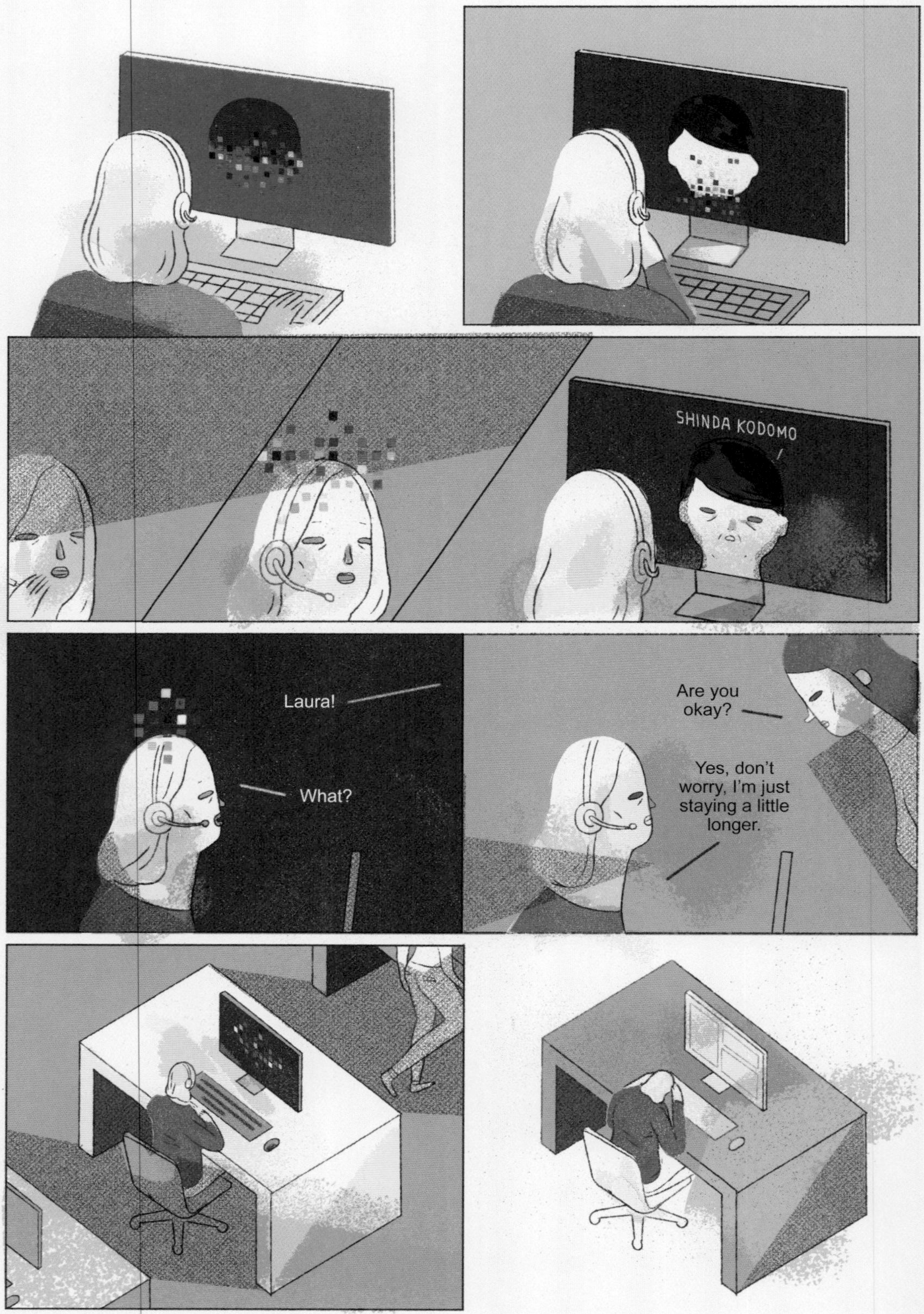
SHINDA KODOMO
Laura!
What?
Are you okay?
Yes, don't worry, I'm just staying a little longer.

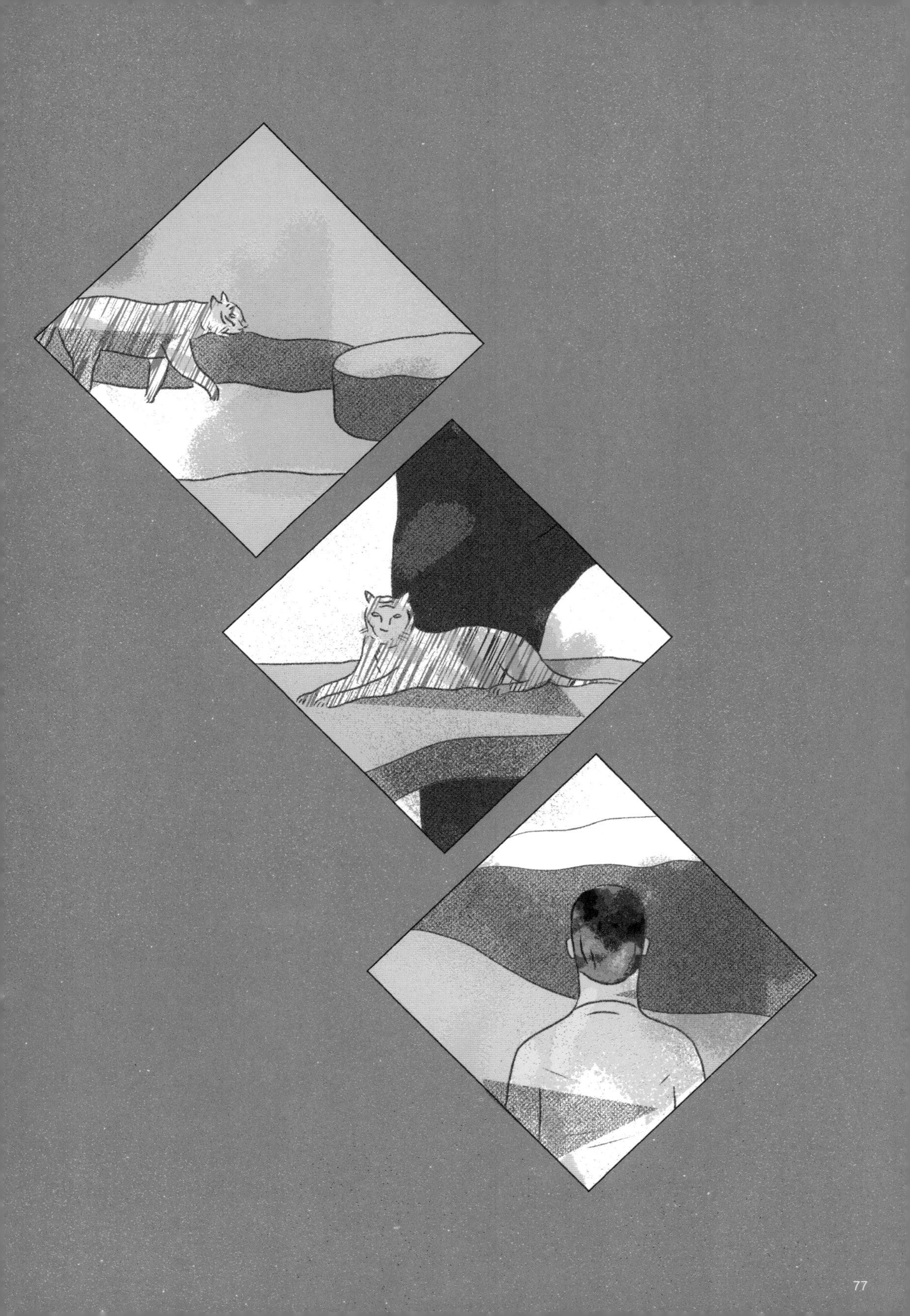

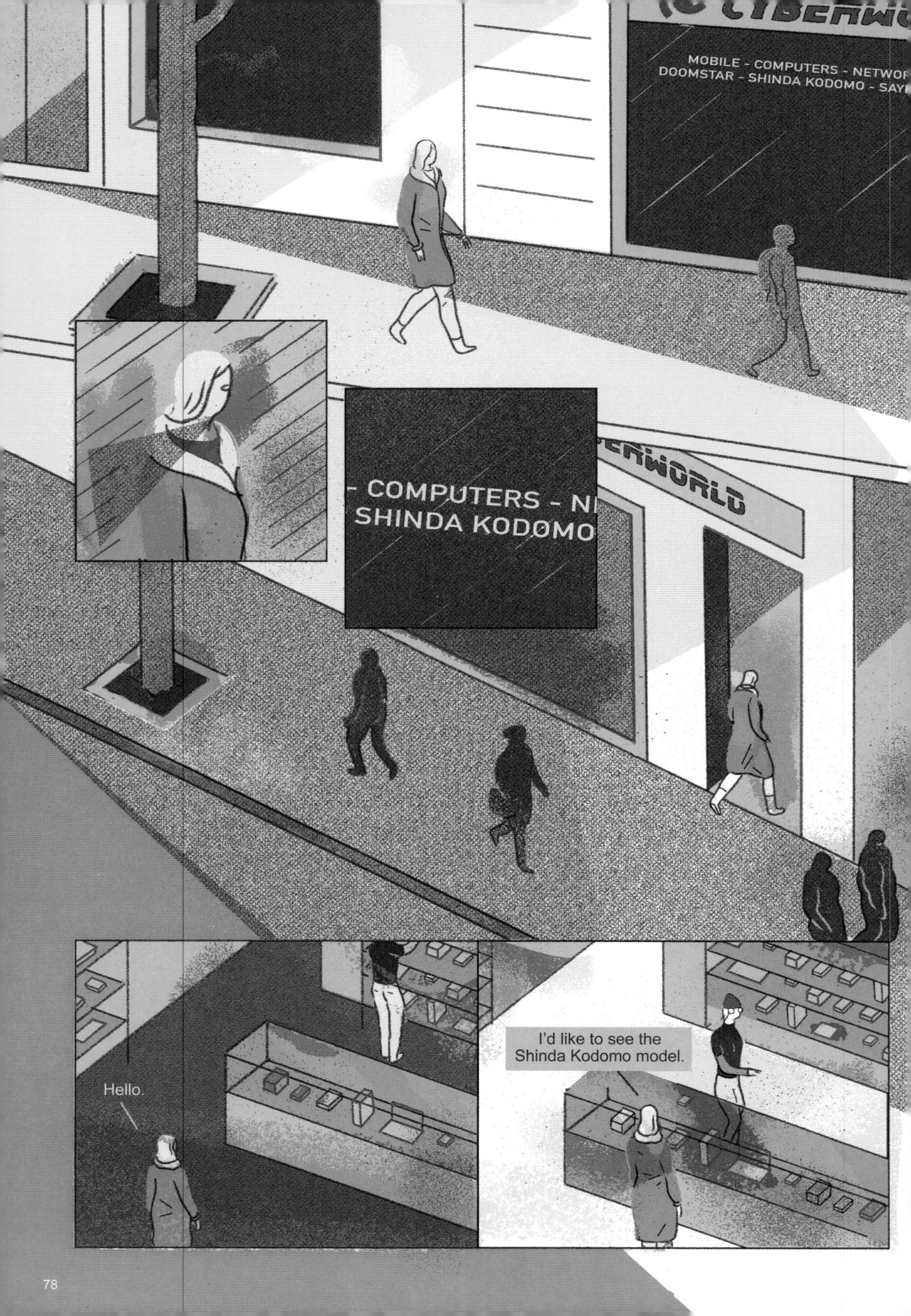

MOBILE - COMPUTERS - NETWOR
DOOMSTAR - SHINDA KODOMO - SAY
- COMPUTERS - N
SHINDA KODOMO
ERWORLD
Hello.
I'd like to see the Shinda Kodomo model.

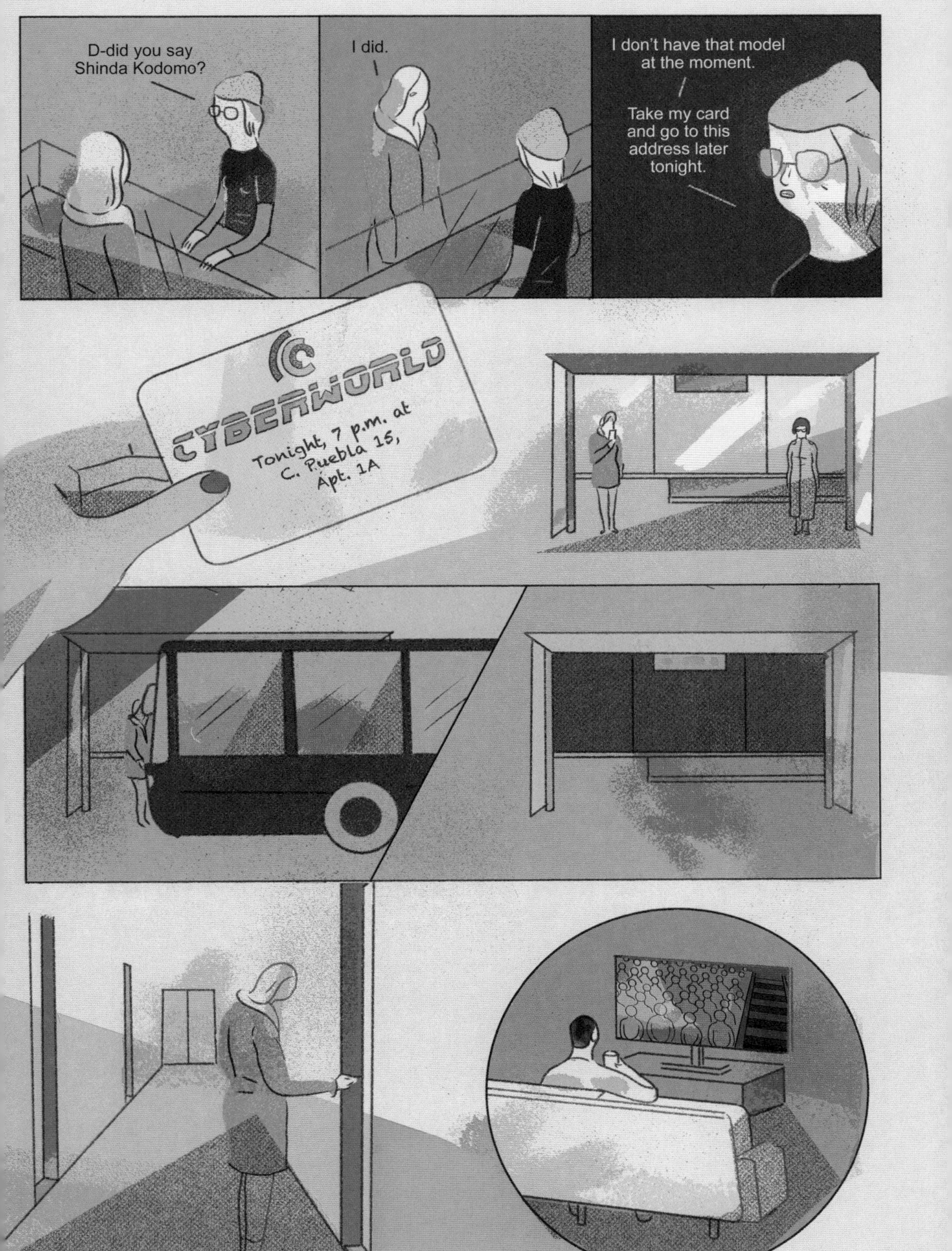
D-did you say Shinda Kodomo?
I did.
I don't have that model at the moment.
Take my card and go to this address later tonight.
CYBERWORLD
Tonight, 7 p.m. at C. Puebla 15, Apt. 1A

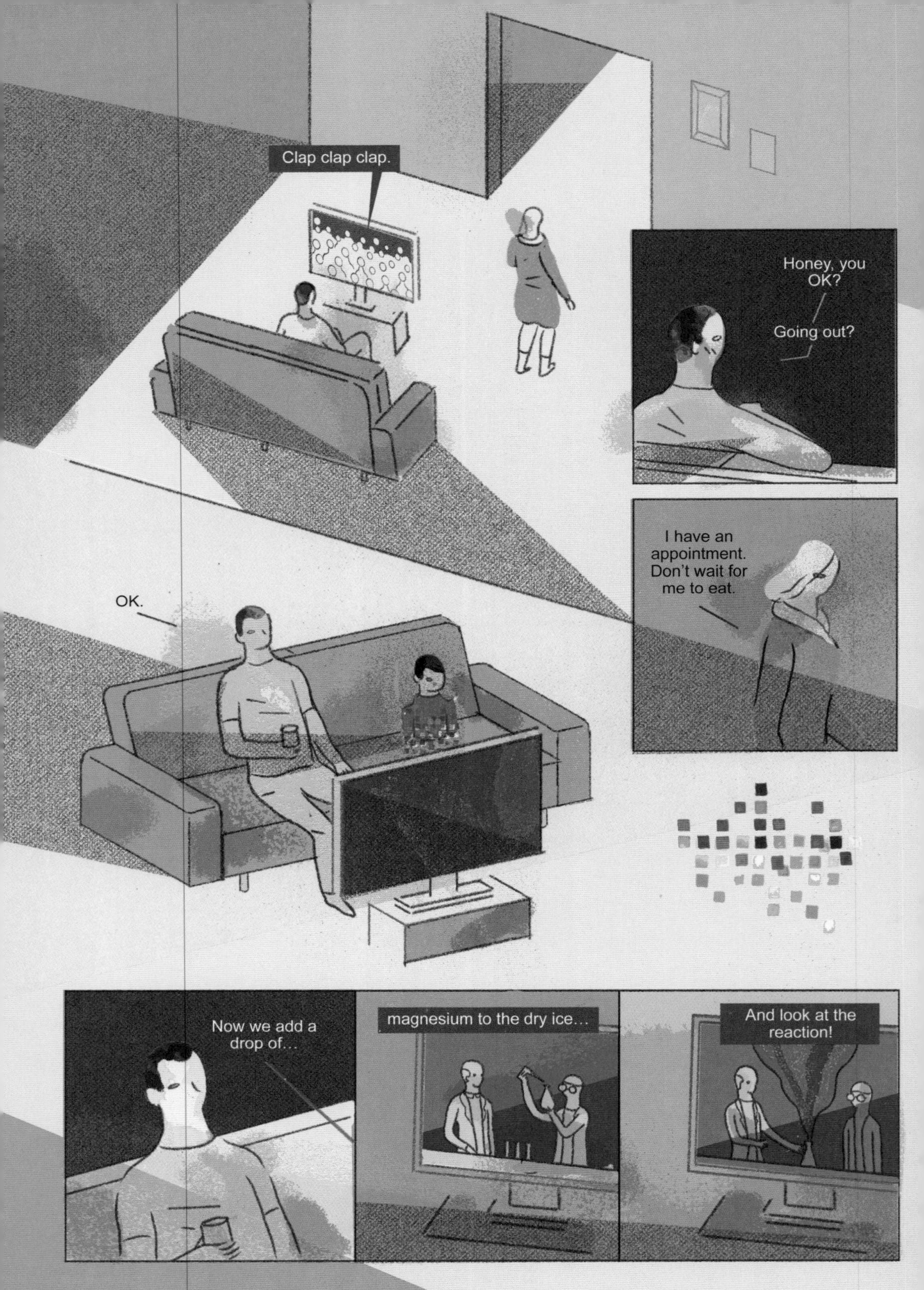
Clap clap clap.
Honey, you OK?
Going out?
I have an appointment. Don't wait for me to eat.
OK.
Now we add a drop of…
magnesium to the dry ice…
And look at the reaction!

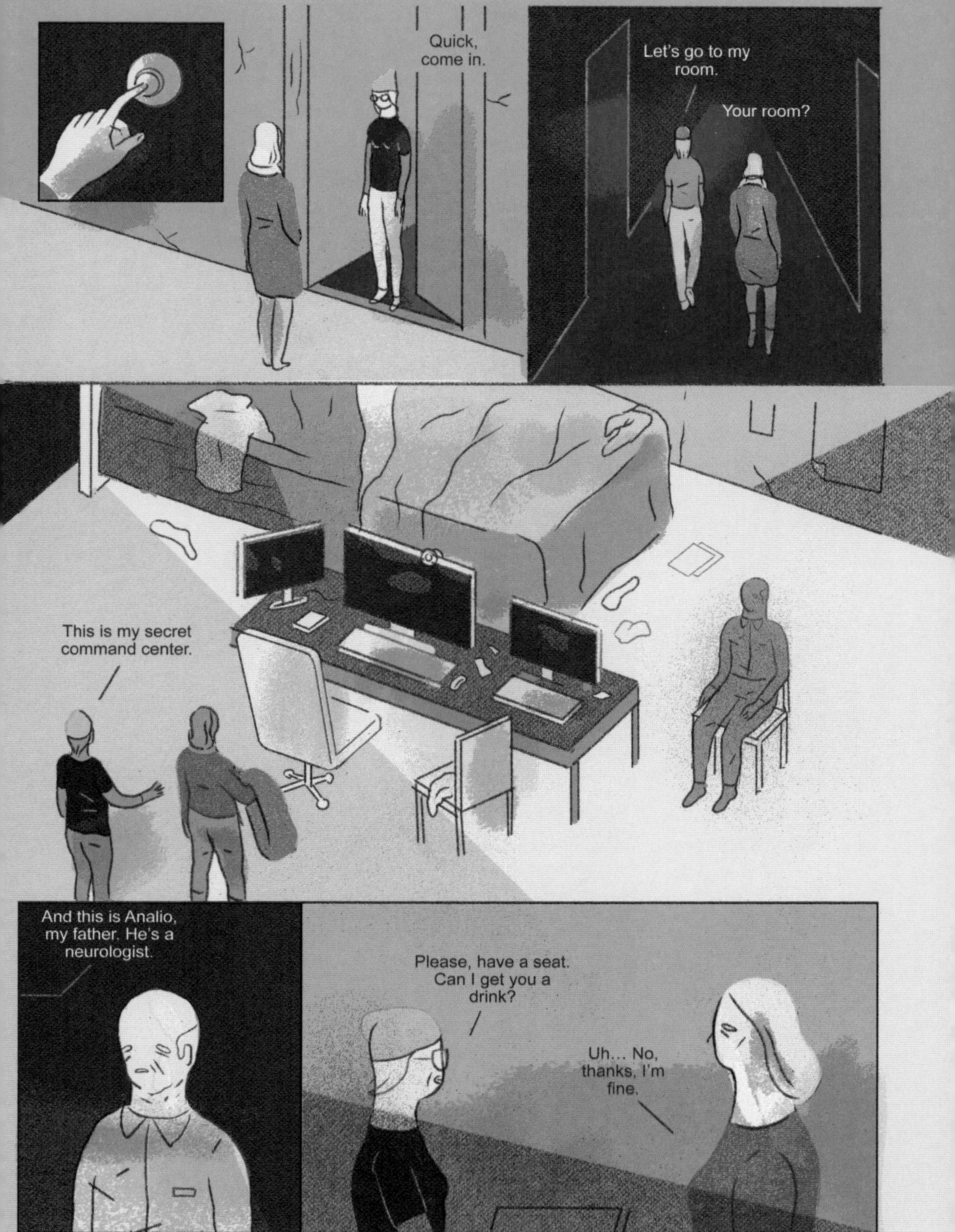
Quick, come in.
Let's go to my room.
Your room?
This is my secret command center.
And this is Analio, my father. He's a neurologist.
Please, have a seat. Can I get you a drink?
Uh… No, thanks, I'm fine.

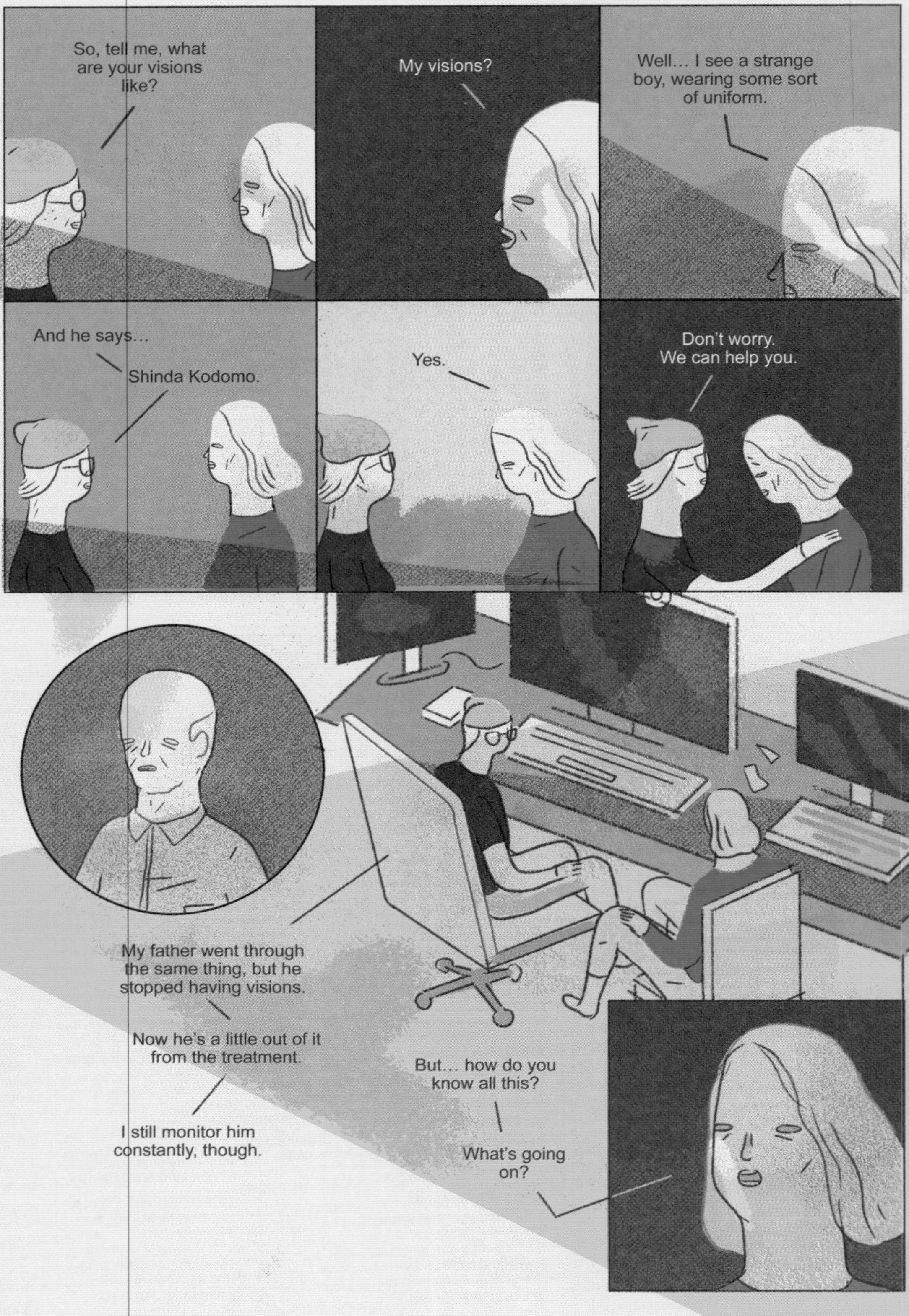

So, tell me, what are your visions like?
My visions?
Well… I see a strange boy, wearing some sort of uniform.
And he says…
Shinda Kodomo.
Yes.
Don't worry. We can help you.
My father went through the same thing, but he stopped having visions.
Now he's a little out of it from the treatment.
I still monitor him constantly, though.
But… how do you know all this?
What's going on?

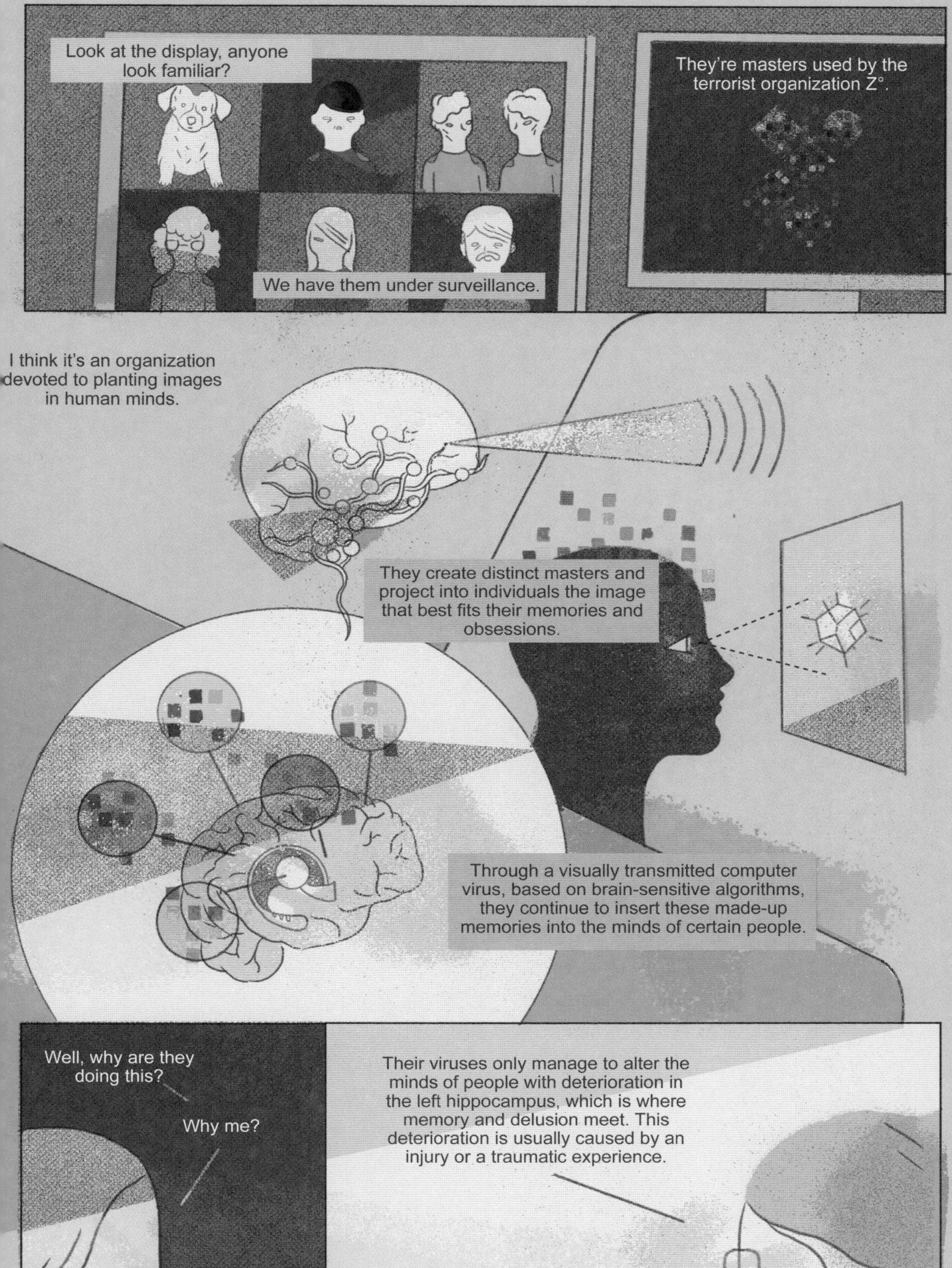

Look at the display, anyone look familiar?
We have them under surveillance.
They're masters used by the terrorist organization Z°.
I think it's an organization devoted to planting images in human minds.
They create distinct masters and project into individuals the image that best fits their memories and obsessions.
Through a visually transmitted computer virus, based on brain-sensitive algorithms, they continue to insert these made-up memories into the minds of certain people.
Well, why are they doing this?
Why me?
Their viruses only manage to alter the minds of people with deterioration in the left hippocampus, which is where memory and delusion meet. This deterioration is usually caused by an injury or a traumatic experience.

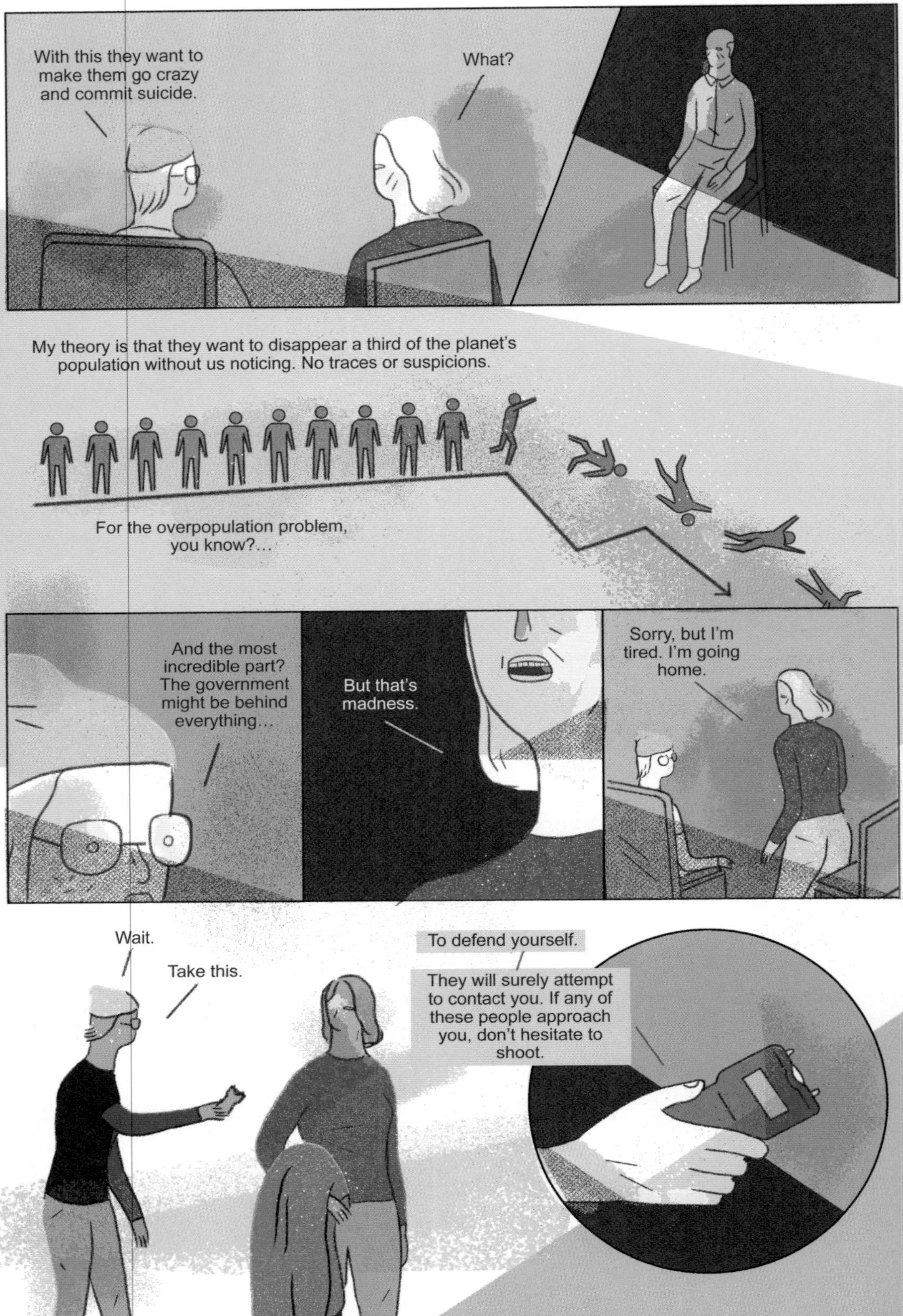
With this they want to make them go crazy and commit suicide.
What?
My theory is that they want to disappear a third of the planet's population without us noticing. No traces or suspicions.
For the overpopulation problem, you know?...
And the most incredible part? The government might be behind everything...
But that's madness.
Sorry, but I'm tired. I'm going home.
Wait.
Take this.
To defend yourself.
They will surely attempt to contact you. If any of these people approach you, don't hesitate to shoot.

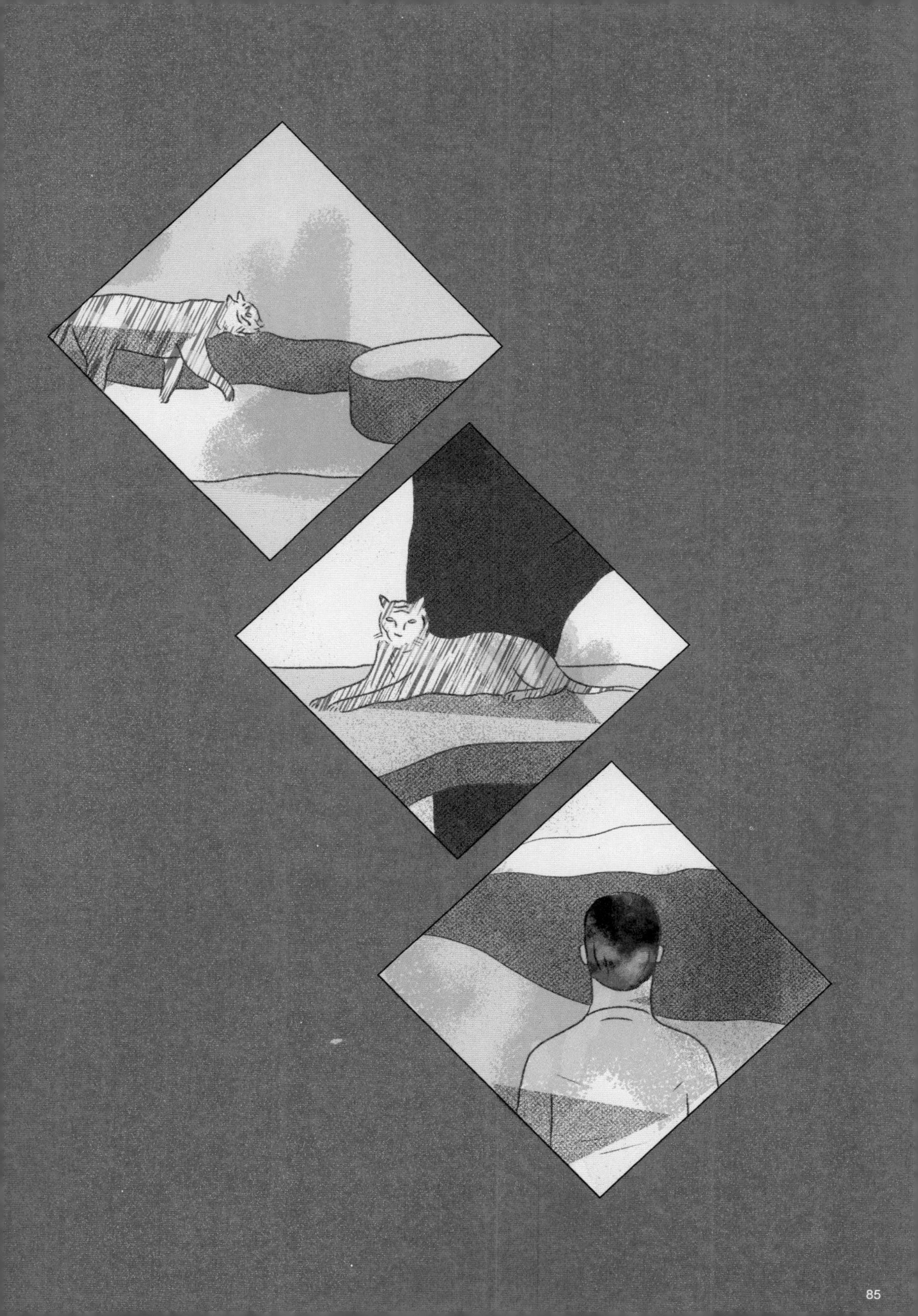

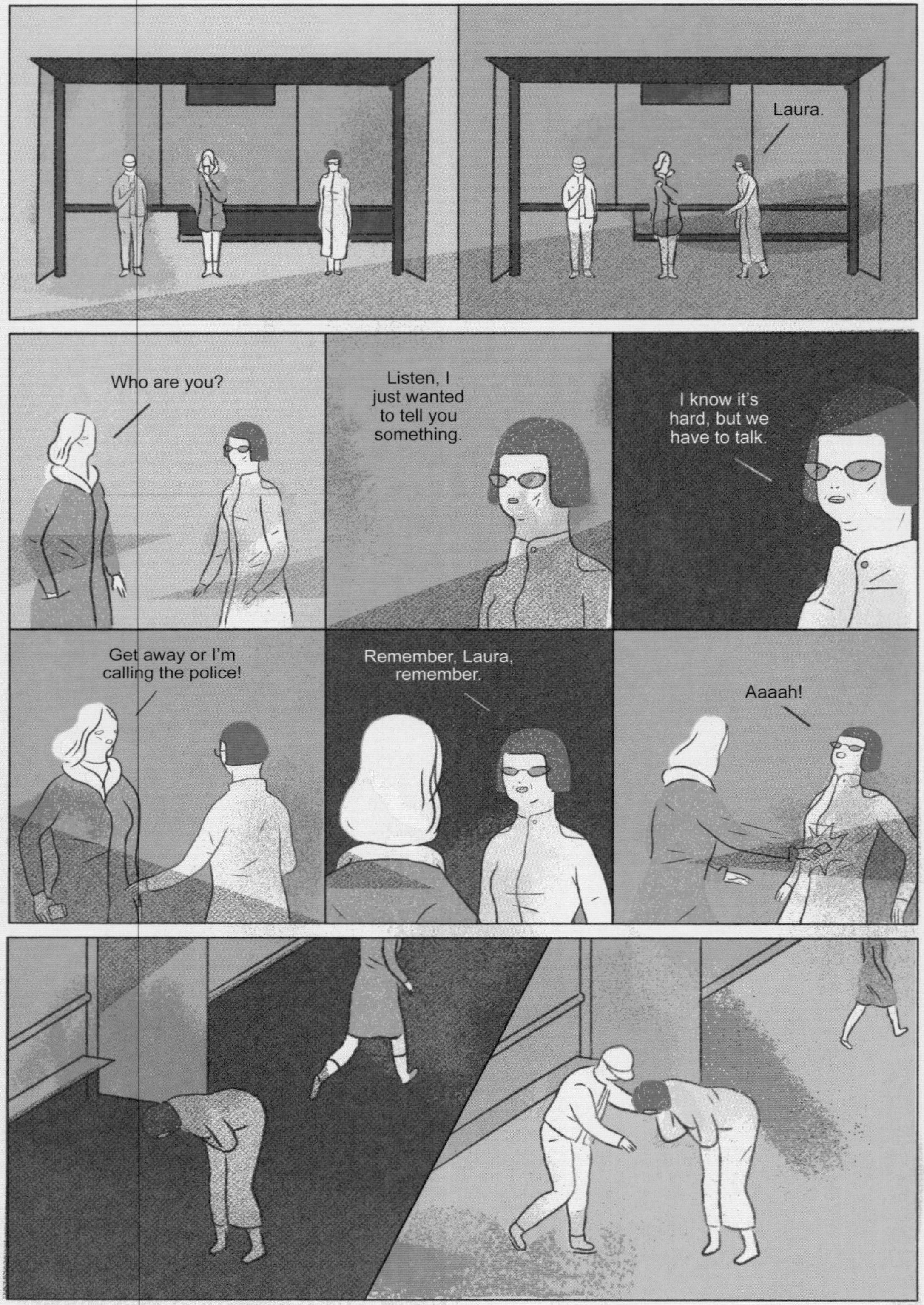
Laura.
Who are you?
Listen, I just wanted to tell you something.
I know it's hard, but we have to talk.
Get away or I'm calling the police!
Remember, Laura, remember.
Aaaah!

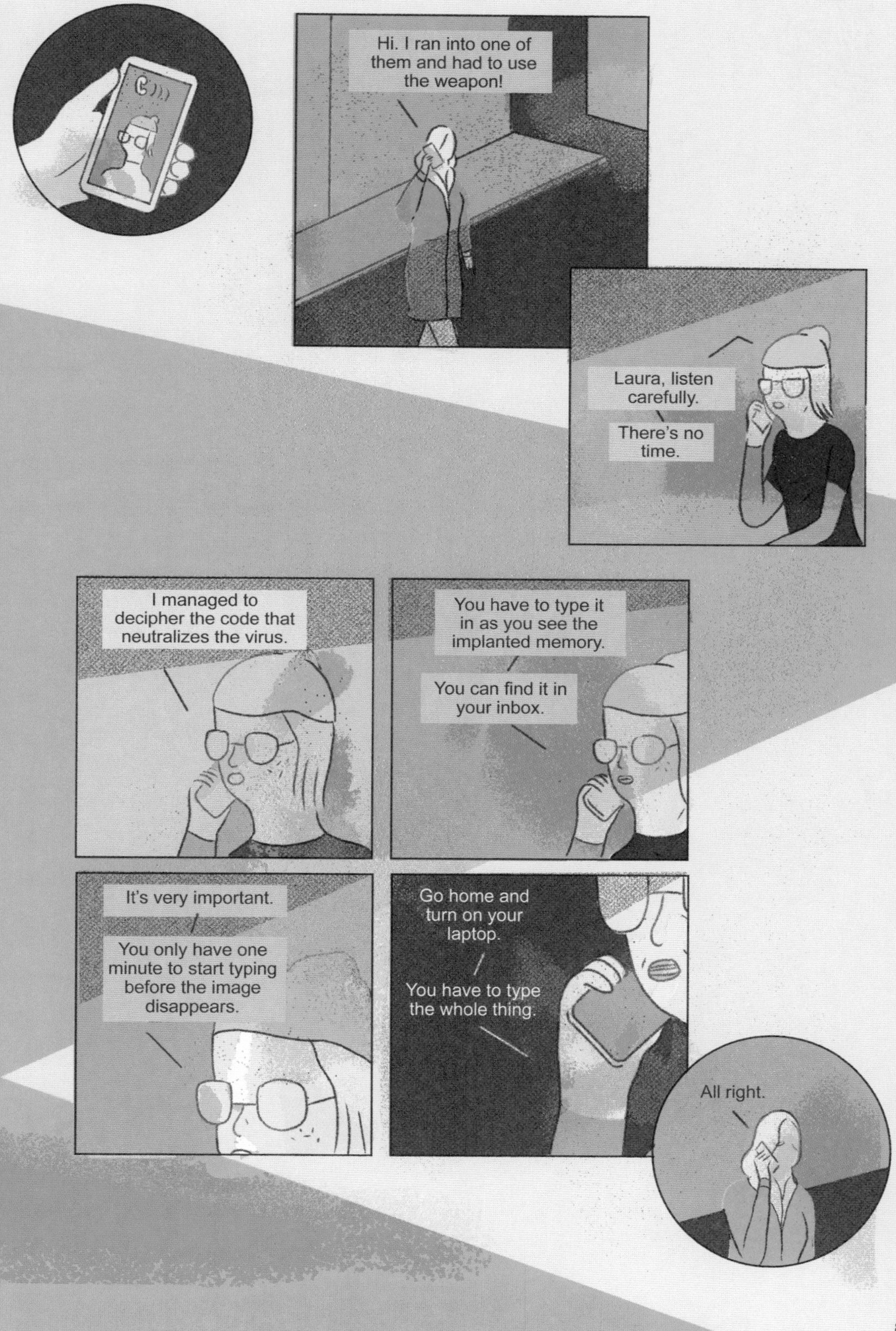

Hi. I ran into one of them and had to use the weapon!
Laura, listen carefully.
There's no time.
I managed to decipher the code that neutralizes the virus.
You have to type it in as you see the implanted memory.
You can find it in your inbox.
It's very important.
You only have one minute to start typing before the image disappears.
Go home and turn on your laptop.
You have to type the whole thing.
All right.

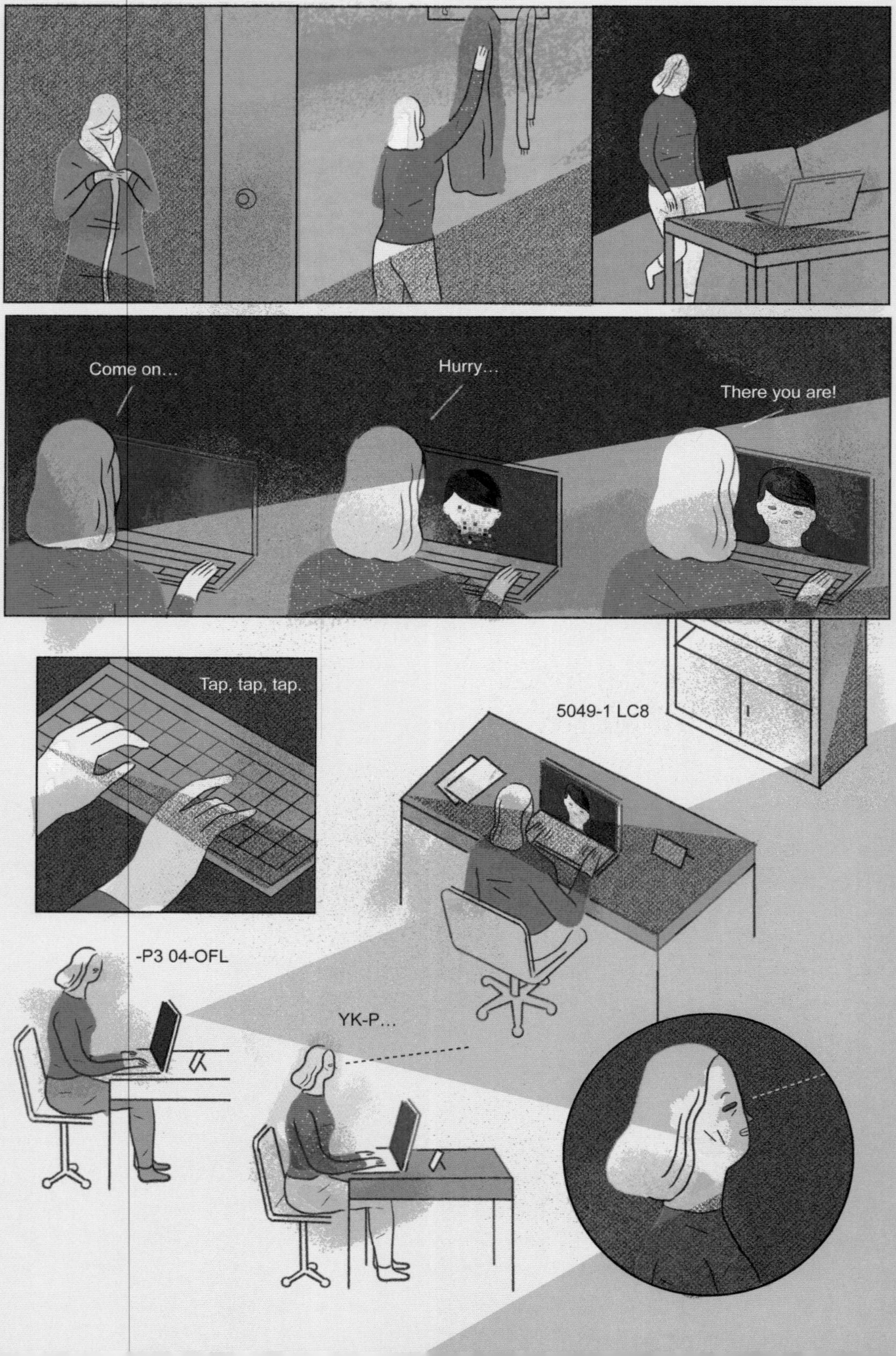

Come on...
Hurry...
There you are!
Tap, tap, tap.
5049-1 LC8
-P3 04-OFL
YK-P...

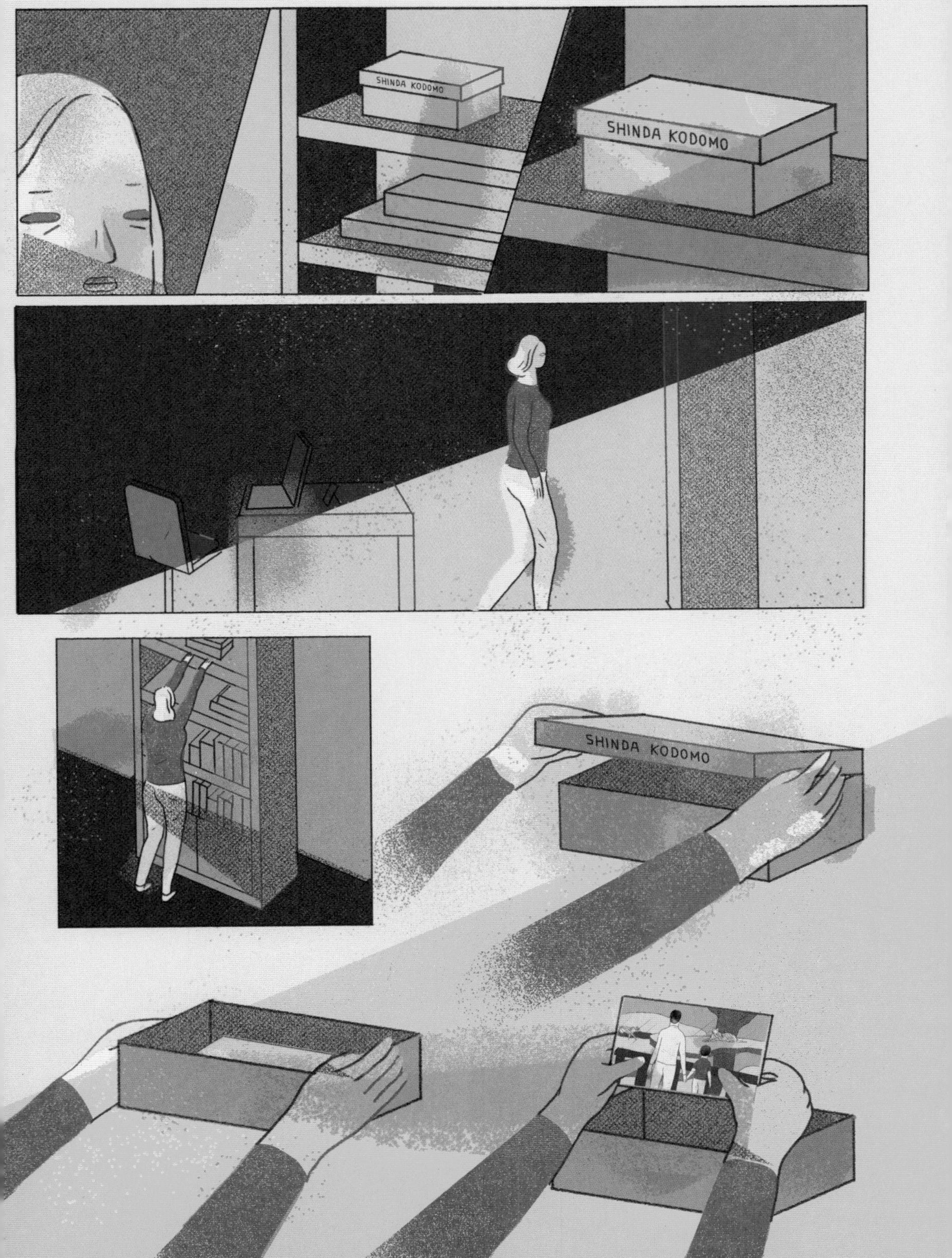
SHINDA KODOMO
SHINDA KODOMO
SHINDA KODOMO

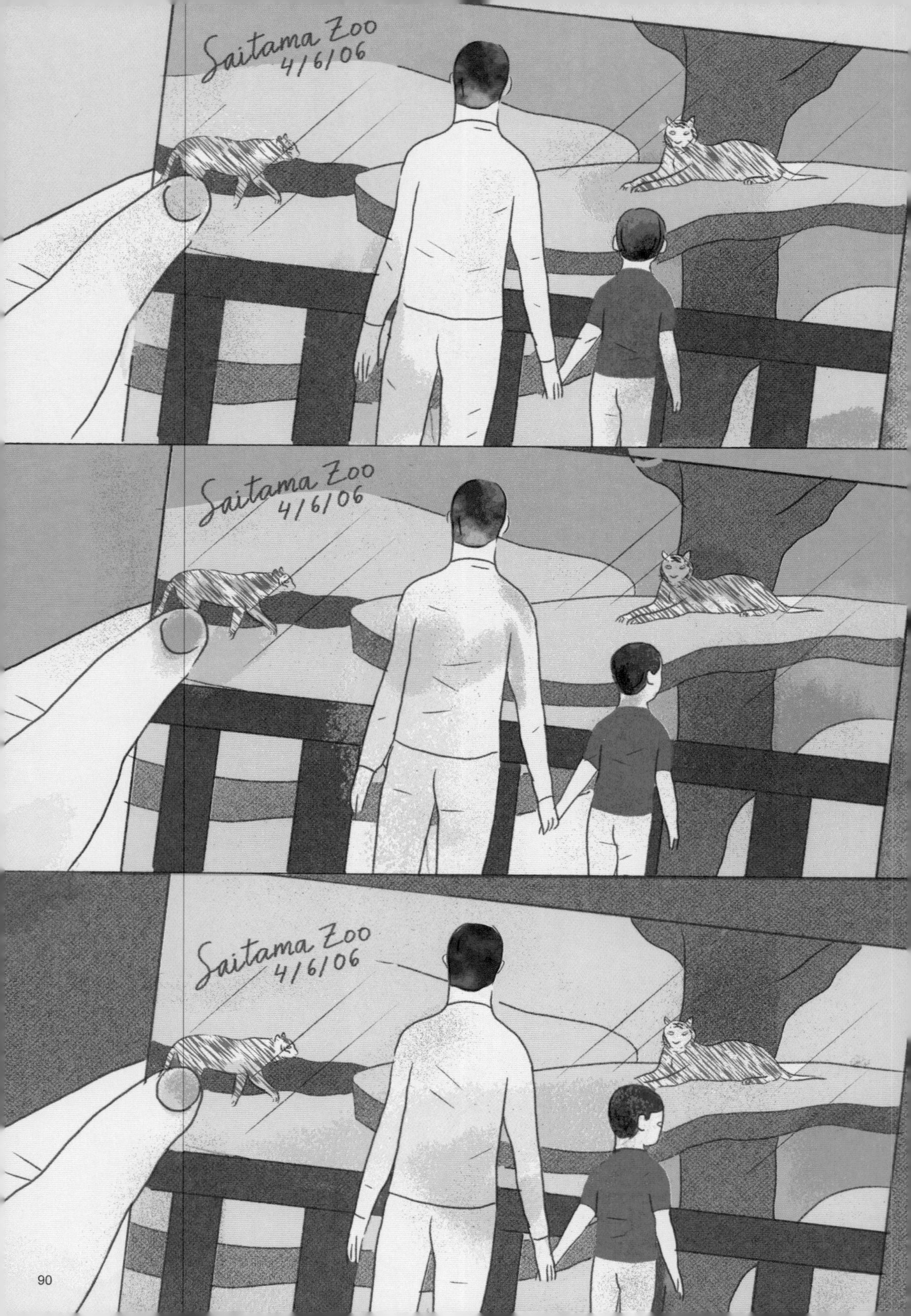
Saitama Zoo
4/6/06
Saitama Zoo
4/6/06
Saitama Zoo
4/6/06

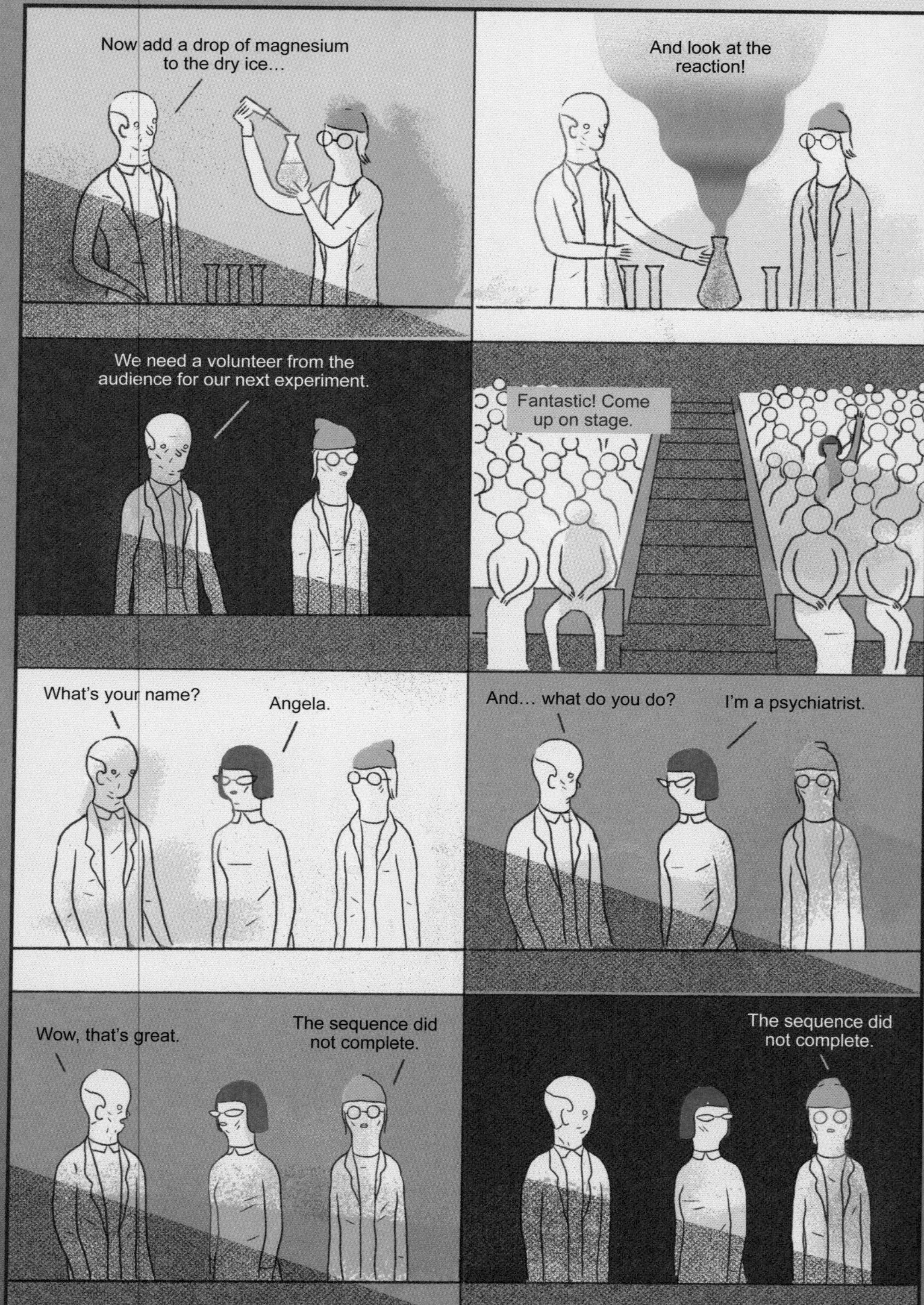
Now add a drop of magnesium to the dry ice…
And look at the reaction!
We need a volunteer from the audience for our next experiment.
Fantastic! Come up on stage.
What's your name?
Angela.
And… what do you do?
I'm a psychiatrist.
Wow, that's great.
The sequence did not complete.
The sequence did not complete.

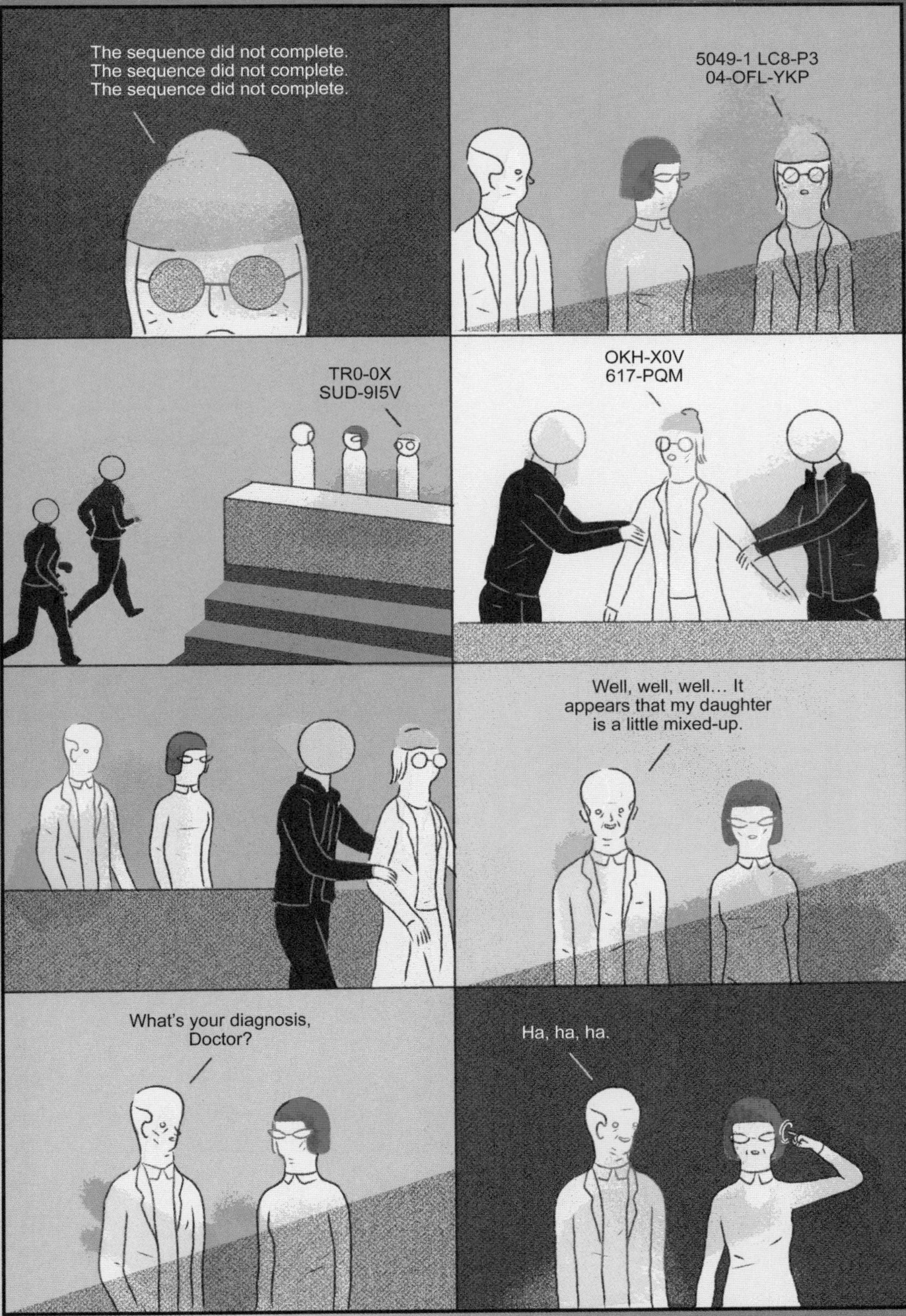
The sequence did not complete.
The sequence did not complete.
The sequence did not complete.
5049-1 LC8-P3
04-OFL-YKP
TR0-0X
SUD-9I5V
OKH-X0V
617-PQM
Well, well, well... It appears that my daughter is a little mixed-up.
What's your diagnosis, Doctor?
Ha, ha, ha.

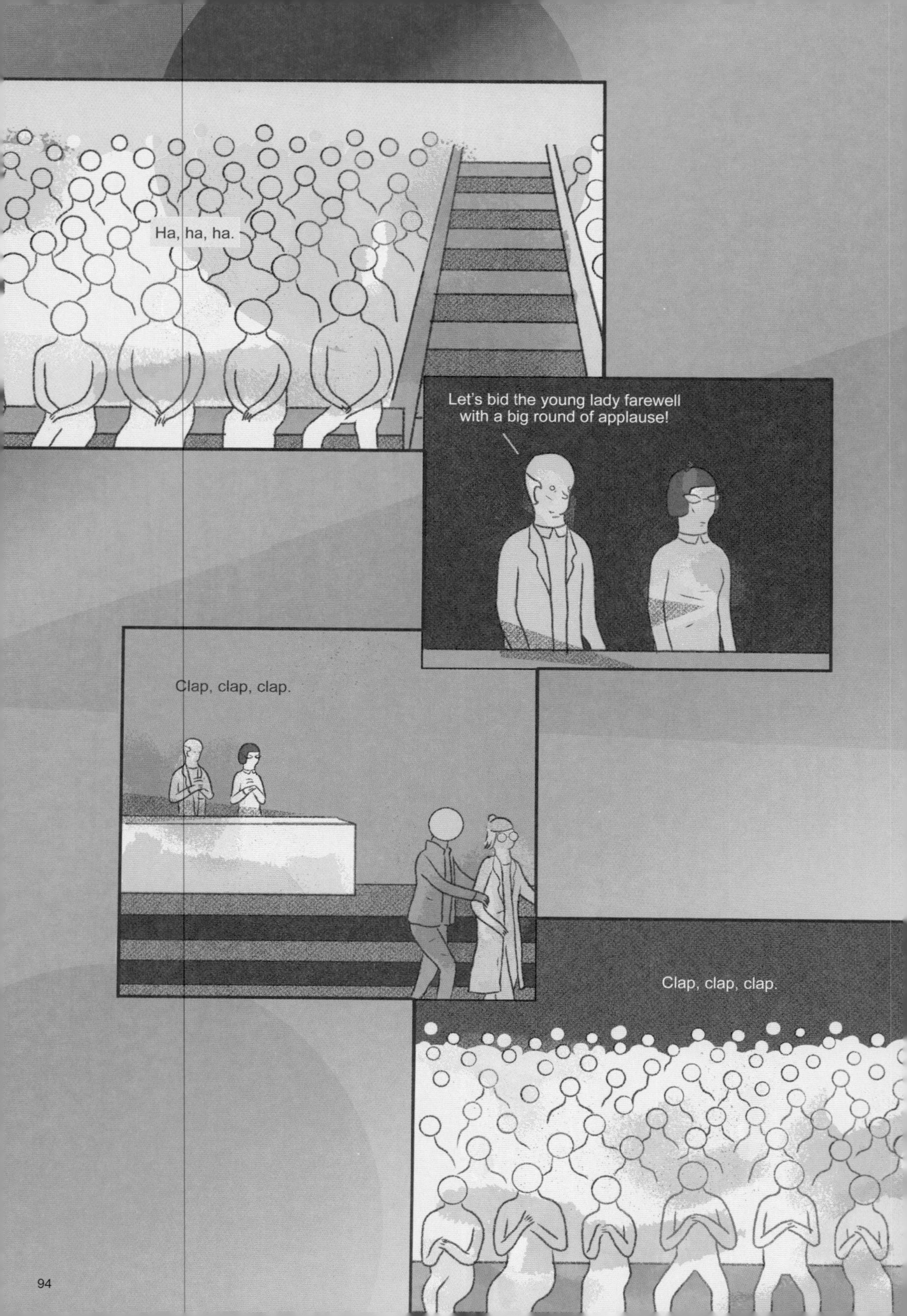
Ha, ha, ha.
Let's bid the young lady farewell with a big round of applause!
Clap, clap, clap.
Clap, clap, clap.

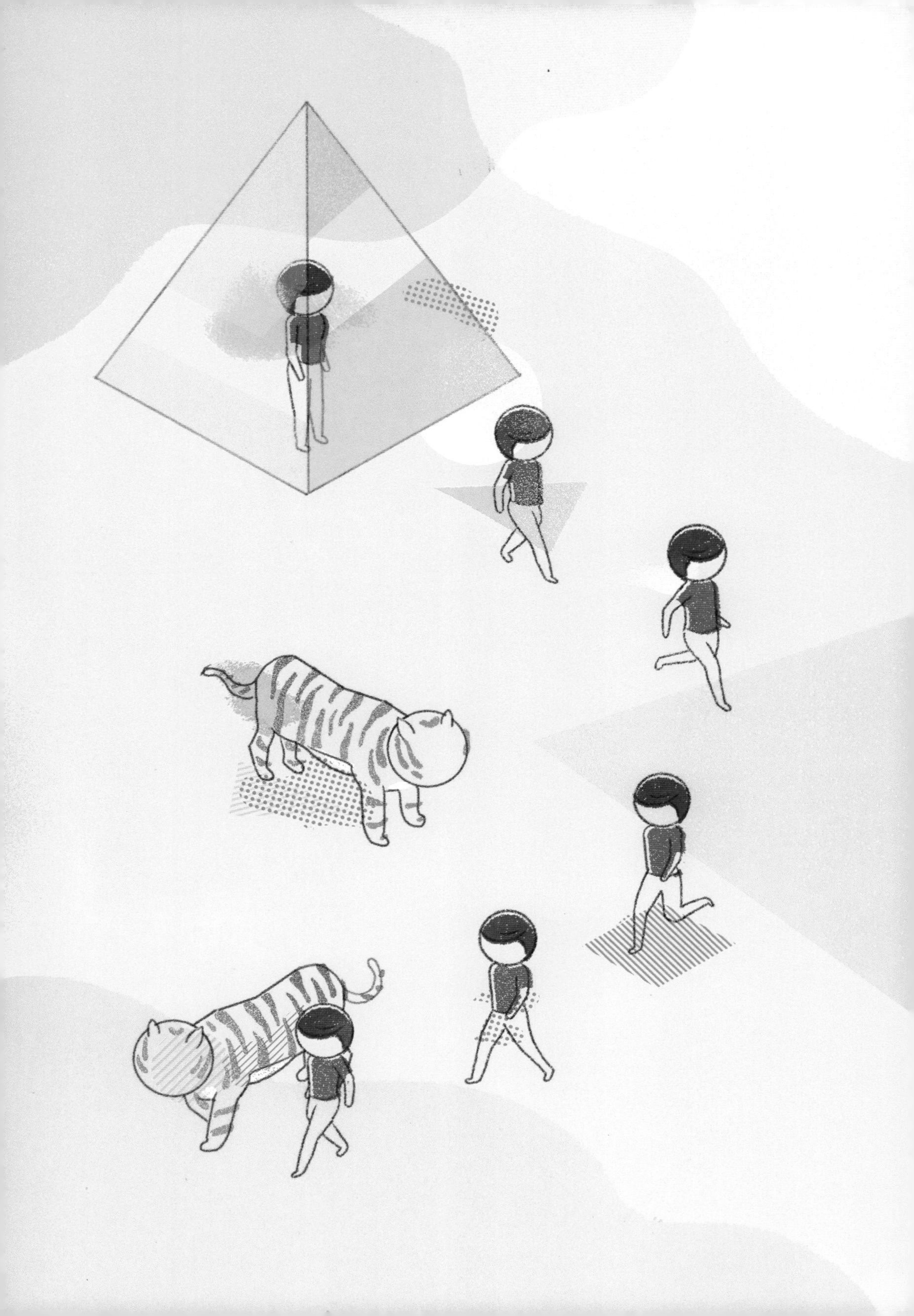

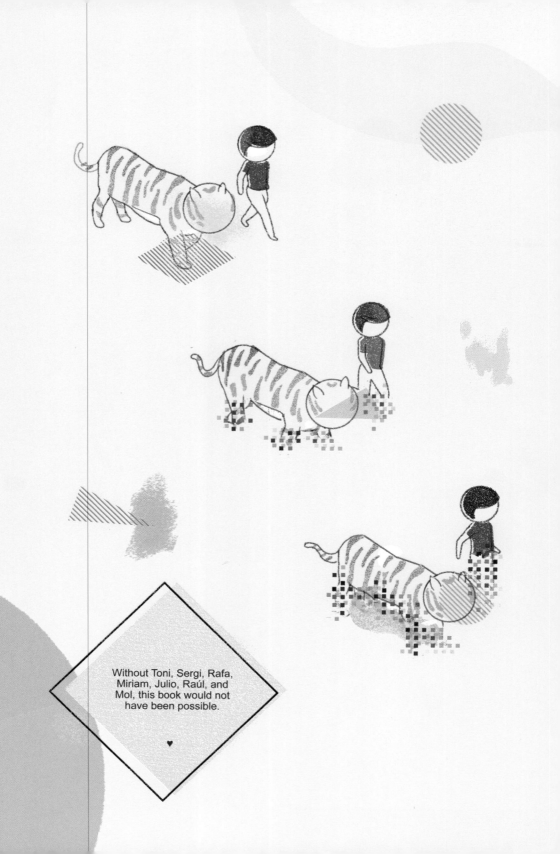

Without Toni, Sergi, Rafa, Miriam, Julio, Raúl, and Mol, this book would not have been possible.

♥